FIGHTING
DEVIL'S
BACKBONE

THE SHADOW OF E.Z.'S FEAR

BOOK ONE

TONY L. TURNBOW

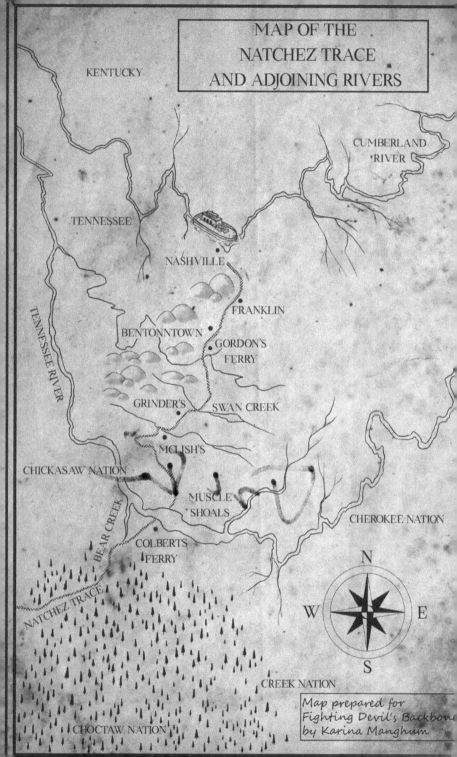

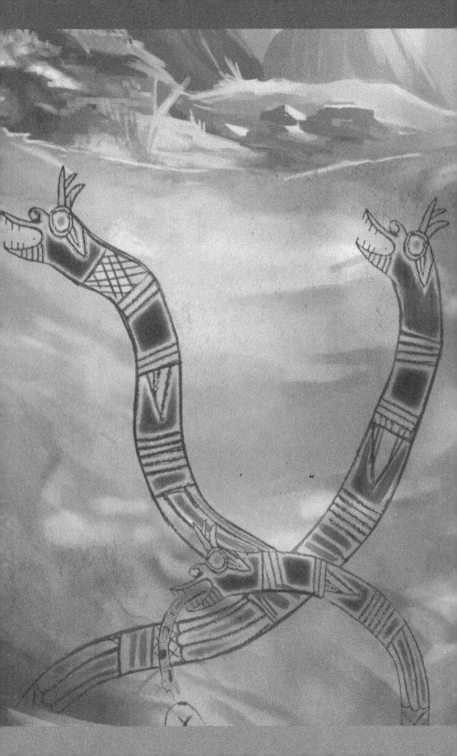

Library of Congress No. 2021903528

ISBN: 978-1-7362608-0-7

This book is fiction. Events and characters depicted in this book are fictitious. Other than historical figures referenced in this book, any similarity to actual persons, living or dead, is purely coincidental.

With credit to Michael Hutzel and FoxFuel Creative, LLC for the cover design, Hanson Suhendra for interior illustrations, Karina Manghum for creating the Natchez Trace map of E. Z.'s world, and Dan Crissman for editing.

With thanks to Nathan Spiess, who suggested that I write this series, and to all who read drafts of the manuscript and provided comments and suggestions.

Contents

Chapter 1—The Boatman   1

Chapter 2—Nashville   10

Chapter 3—Chosen   25

Chapter 4—The Mysterious Mr. Burton   33

Chapter 5—The Escape   44

Chapter 6—The Map   57

Chapter 7—The Test   70

Chapter 8—Bentontown   78

Chapter 9—The Gate to the Wilderness   87

Chapter 10—Snakes   101

Chapter 11—Swan Creek   113

Chapter 12—The Ghost Cave   122

Chapter 13—The Spaniard   131

Chapter 14—The Baron   149

Chapter 15—Chickasaw Friends   164

Chapter 16—Jack, the Bully   179

Chapter 17—Sinking Creek Militia   192

Chapter 18—Torches   200

Chapter 19—Crossing the River   214

Chapter 20—Transition to a New World   231

Chapter 21—Tomorrow   237

Author's Note   243

About the Author   246

THE SHADOW OF E. Z.'S FEAR

CHAPTER ONE

The Boatman

On the Cumberland River in Tennessee, 1809

A gnarled hand, missing a thumb, reached from behind a crate on the boat and clenched the boy's shoulder hard enough to hurt. "The Devil's Backbone," croaked a whisper from a foul odor just behind his ear.

Startled, the boy pulled away in revulsion but said nothing.

"That's where this boat's a'takin you, 'The Devil's Backbone.' It will fight you. And no one will ever hear from you again!"

The old boatman had caught the boy, E. Z. Perkins, alone. He warned about the mysterious trail where the boy was headed. It was the Natchez Trace, the ancient path that ran from Nashville, deep into Indian territory. The forest it passed through was so dark and unknown that travelers called it "The Wilderness." The trail itself was so dangerous it had earned the name "The Devil's Backbone."

The boatman warned that land pirates and robbers could cut the boy open and fill him with stones to hide his body in swamps. Indian warriors could torture him for hours with hot knives before cutting off his scalp.

If those tales were not enough to frighten E. Z., the boatman told supernatural stories of giant, black, hairy creatures that hid along the wilderness road. As travelers passed by the creatures' hiding places, the creatures jumped on travelers' backs and fought them.

The old man's faded, steel-blue eyes looked as if the sun had bleached them white. And they danced wild as he talked, suggesting that he had seen things he wanted to describe but could not find the words.

No one noticed that the boy was trapped where the boatman had cornered him. E. Z. could shout for help or try to dart around the old man.

What held him were the stories. If the old man intended to captivate the boy, it worked. E. Z. did not want to run. He wanted to know all about the dangers ahead from someone who had been there and who had lived to tell about them.

Finally, the boat captain shouted at the old man to get back to work. The boatman took off a small hunting bag hanging from his shoulder on a leather strap and handed it to E. Z.

"Here. This bag has survived journeys like yours on the Natchez Trace."

The dark brown bag with a small flap on front was made of deer skin and was soft. But it was stained from earlier journeys on the road. Some stains appeared to be from blood.

The boatman smiled as E. Z. studied the blood. He stepped forward to a few inches from E. Z.'s face, "Keep it with you. You'll need it. You'll see."

E. Z. stepped backwards. "Thank you." Escaping the boatman's spell, E. Z. climbed a ladder to the roof of the boat.

E. Z. hoped the roof perch would help him scout a first glimpse of Nashville. He had heard the lookout shout the name of the town when they had arrived at their previous stop at Clarksville. This time, he planned to beat the scout to the first sighting and become the crewmen's hero.

The wooden keelboat, weighed down with passengers and cargo, floated lazily along steep bluffs beside the Cumberland River. The boat was rough, more like a floating barn, with a flat wooden bottom and large wooden shelter built on top.

Willow trees hung over the water. Their bendy limbs waived like curtains in the hot summer breeze, hiding any dangers around the next turn. The whole effect was so peaceful it was hypnotic.

But it was an illusion. The float only seemed lazy. Just below the surface, an unseen river current pushed back against the boat, as if nature were trying to push the passengers back home where they belonged, back home where it was safe.

Frontier boatmen, crusted with a week's sweat and dirt, struggled against it. They wrestled the water with long cane poles to find the bottom of the river. Then, they pushed against it with all their strength to propel the boat ahead to where the river naturally would not have taken them.

"E. Z.," pronounced "Easy," was the nickname his brother David had given him. It was short for "Ezekiel." E. Z. was anything but short at almost six feet tall, unusually tall for a boy his age.

E. Z. was growing fast, and he was thin and awkward. E. Z.'s mother Sarah often said that he was so thin a high wind could blow him away. Once, as a storm approached, E. Z. tried jumping with the wind at his back, but he still could not take flight.

E. Z. remembered his mother's warning as the breeze grew into a stronger wind that pushed at his back. Gusts grew strong enough that E. Z. held onto a railing to avoid falling off into the river.

The wind provided cool relief from the sticky summer heat. The river released a sweet scent in the hot sun, and the breeze carried the aroma up to the boat and swirled around him.

E. Z. suspected that the sweet aroma was another river illusion to lull him into ignoring the dangers. Boatmen had told him stories about boys being pulled under by river currents as they swam in the Cumberland. Currents, they said, were unseen arms that reached up and yanked unsuspecting boys down to the murky depths of the river to drown them.

As E. Z. explored the flat roof, he overheard boatmen below talking about his family. His mother had brought the boys without their father. Anyone could see that the three of them were alone on this journey into the unknown.

"It pains me to see it, it does," a burly man said. "Whoever heard of sech a thin'? Them boys know nothin' about survivin' The Devil's Backbone. They'll die turrible deaths on it, and their mother with 'em. She has no idea what she's gettin' 'em into."

"'Sheep to the slaughter,' is what I say. It'll kill 'em shore as I'm standin' here," another man agreed.

E. Z. worked to ignore a growing fear by looking for diversions to fill his thoughts. He stood on his toes to try to look beyond the next bend. It was a moment of pride when he realized he was the highest thing on the boat — "King of the Boat," he imagined.

Then E. Z.'s hair began standing straight up on end above his head. A strange tingle ran up his leg and into his back.

KERPOW!

A blinding lightning bolt shot out of the sky, splitting a tree apart and setting it on fire on the bluff near the boat. Small balls of green fire from the lightning bounced along the ground and fell into the river. Puffs of steam marked their watery graves.

"That could've been you!" one of the steersmen yelled from below. "Get inside before you get fried up like a chicken in a pot! River water draws lightnin'!"

The steersman looked at the burly man. "Yo're right. That boy don't know nothin' but the town life in the East."

E. Z. climbed down and ran inside the boat just in time. Heavy black clouds rolled in fast and turned the afternoon sky so dark that it appeared to be night. Inside the boat was even darker.

When the steersmen followed E. Z. inside, he began to worry. Those were the only men guiding the boat. The captain slammed the door shut and commanded the crewmen to stand near the edge of the room all the way around to help balance the boat. It made no sense to E. Z. The boat was steady.

Suddenly, a wall of rain hit the boat from the side. It listed sideways at an angle. Three people fell. Wind whipped and rocked the boat so hard that E. Z. thought it might turn upside down. He could swim, but his brother David could not.

The boat leveled again. But then it began a constant rocking as the wind shifted from different directions. E. Z. maneuvered through the darkness to find David.

E. Z. was not sure he could pull David's weight out of the water, but maybe he could show him how to stay afloat. David was shorter than E. Z. and pudgy. He was five years younger. Their mother Sarah often said that David's body was storing up fat for when he started to grow. Then he would be big and strong.

E. Z. caught a glimpse of David's shape. Few people suspected that the two were brothers. It was not only their shapes and sizes that were different. E. Z.'s hair was sandy brown. David's was bright red with a cowlick that made his hair shoot up from the back.

E. Z. handed David the hunting bag to carry his drawing tablet. Sarah had bought David a drawing tablet to record images of their trip. David was prone to worry, and the tablet was his mother's attempt to take his mind off the dangers. Following his mother's example, E. Z. attempted to distract his brother from the storm rocking the boat.

"Where did you get this?" David asked. "It looks like a soldier's."

"One of the boatmen gave it to me," E. Z. said. "He told me to keep it. I don't know why. There's nothing in it. I thought you could use it."

"Soldiers put their ammunition in these bags. I don't have any," David said.

"Soldiers put whatever they need to carry in them. Keep your drawing tablet and charcoal in it," E. Z. said.

Booming thunder shook the boat. Babies began to cry in the dark, and a crewman lit a candle to give light.

In the glow of the candle, dark spots on the bag stood out. "What are those?" David asked.

"Spots. Maybe it was carried in a battle. The boatman said that this bag has survived journeys like ours on the Natchez Trace," E. Z. said.

David held the bag close to examine it. E. Z. did not fool him. David put the bag down when he realized the spots were blood. David asked, "Did the man who carried it survive too?"

Staring at bloodstains in the rocking boat made David's face turn green. He bolted toward the door to throw up off the side of the boat. E. Z. grabbed David by the shirt and pulled him back in. "Some boatman you're going to be," he said.

David said, "I don't want to be a sailor. I want to be a soldier."

"You'll get a chance to be a soldier soon enough," E. Z. said. "The captain told me that we may meet Creek or Shawnee Indians on the Natchez Trace. If we get attacked, everybody has to fight."

David stared at the floor.

E. Z. said, "Some of the boatmen told me stories about what Indians do to children. They smiled at each other. I don't know whether to believe them."

E. Z. wanted to prepare his brother for the dangers ahead. David had such a vivid imagination, though. E. Z. dared not tell him the boatman's stories about the hairy creatures. Especially while it was dark.

David's eyes widened and teared. "Where's Ma?" he asked.

"She's on the other side of the room holding a baby for that woman who has too many to handle," E. Z. said.

E. Z. put his hand on David's shoulder, but not to comfort him as he had when his brother was smaller. This time he was stern. "You'd better not cry. Or I'll wallop you."

David was not convinced. "I want to go back home."

"We don't have a home back in Pennsylvania anymore. Ma has told you. Our new home is somewhere down the Natchez Trace. It's going to be up to us to help her find it."

David flipped the paper in his drawing tablet, pretending not to hear.

The boatmen's predictions of doom worried E. Z., and he pressed on. "Look," E. Z. said, "We don't have anybody to do it for us. I don't know what all we'll face before we get there, so you have to do your part, or we won't make it."

"Ma promised it would be an adventure. You're enjoying it. I'm not!" David said. David liked the idea of adventure, but he liked it better on paper where he was in control.

"It doesn't matter whether we enjoy it. Ma has decided it's what we should do. Just make the best of it," E. Z. said.

As E. Z. prepared to push his brother into a commitment, the roof of the boat exploded from the deafening sound of pounding hailstones. The wind growled and turned into a high-pitched whine. Boat timbers creaked as if they would break in two.

E. Z. looked across the room to see the wild-eyed boatman staring back and pointing to the roof. He could read his lips saying, "See, it's a'tryin to warn you."

CHAPTER TWO

Nashville

"Nashville, Nashville, Nashville," E. Z.'s voice echoed down the cliffs on the river to add to the effect. He had taken advantage of the quick end of the storm to race back to the roof. It was a moment of satisfaction to watch boatmen follow his lead to catch their first view of the town.

One of the boatmen blew a long, wooden horn to alert men at the wharf to be ready to pull them in. Hearing the signal, other travelers came out to the deck to take in their first glimpse of Nashville on the bluff.

David followed him and pulled out his drawing tablet and charcoal.

"What are you drawing?" E. Z. asked.

David said nothing.

E. Z. glanced over David's shoulder to see that he was drawing a map of the Cumberland River. "You don't need to map our route. We can't go back," E. Z. said as he put the hunting bag strap over David's shoulder.

E. Z. was disappointed that Nashville appeared to be smaller than he had expected. But at least it had a few brick buildings like those back home. Maybe he would have a chance to sleep on one of the porches that night and eat a good meal at one of the inns.

Three black men came out to the edge of the wharf to pull in the boat and to lay the gangplank for travelers to exit. One young boatman chose to jump to the wharf instead to make an impression on young ladies onboard. The captain said something angry to him in words that E. Z. and David had not heard at home.

The boatman with the wild eyes spotted E. Z. from the opposite side of the boat and hurried toward him. E. Z. did not want David to hear the boatman's stories or he would have to drag his brother down the Natchez Trace.

But the Perkins family was stalled. The captain stood at the gangplank speaking to the passengers as they left, wishing them well on whatever the next leg of the trip would be. The boatman caught up to them.

The old boatman's faded eyes had turned red as he stared at E. Z. with anger. "That bag was for you to carry," he said as he reached toward David to pull the bag off his shoulder.

E. Z. pushed David forward around waiting passengers to keep him out of the old man's reach. As the boys ran off the gangplank, passengers' chatter was so loud that E. Z.

only heard the boatman repeat, "No one will ever hear from you again!"

Wagons for hire waited at the end of the gangplank to take passengers' baggage into town. Sarah had packed all the family's belongings into two small, wooden trunks.

E. Z. noticed several of the boatmen tip their hats to his mother as she walked down the gangplank. He did not know why, but their eyes followed the attractive, thin woman with light blond hair.

One of the boatmen on the wharf directed two men to carry Sarah's trunks. He handed a wagon driver a Spanish coin and told him to take the family to the Nashville Inn. Sarah objected. But the boatman walked away tipping his hat, leaving her no choice after the trunks had been loaded.

The teamster offered Sarah a seat next to him on the wagon. To E. Z.'s disappointment, his mother chose instead to walk alongside. She said a little unconvincingly that she needed to walk after being on the boat for so long.

The wagon had barely moved when Sarah's feet began to sink down in the mud and mire of the dirt street after the thunderstorm.

"I can't enter Nashville looking like a muddy street tramp. I suppose we have no choice," Sarah said, and then shouted, "Driver! Stop!"

The Perkins family mounted the wagon and took their places. The driver stared at Sarah and smiled, revealing shiny gums where teeth had once been. He snapped the reins and the horses proceeded on.

E. Z. looked behind to the river, and he saw the boatman with the wild eyes following their wagon at a distance. "Won't your horses go any faster?" he asked the driver.

The driver's gaze was fixed on Sarah, and he paid E. Z. no attention. Fortunately, another teamster pulled a load of cotton across the street just in time to block the boatman.

The wagon rounded the corner, immersing the family into a sea of noise and confusion on Nashville Public Square. It was a Saturday afternoon. Cattlemen drove bellowing herds through the streets to the livestock market across from the Court House. Farmers had come into town to barter their crops in stores. Wagon wheels creaked under heavy loads of farm goods hauled toward the wharves to Rapier and Stump's flatboats bound for Natchez and New Orleans. Street peddlers stood by their wares and barked for people to stop to buy "rare items from Philadelphia, New Orleans, and Paris, France." Or so they said. E. Z. could not imagine seeing anything that had once been in France.

Boys slightly older than E. Z. raced horses through the square as fast as they could. The teenagers had no place to go. They just wanted to show everyone that they could ride fast.

E. Z. pictured himself riding a fast horse into his new town once his family had settled. First, he would have to get a horse. No, first he would have to find their new town and help build their home. The day when he could afford the luxury of a fast horse was too far off to allow himself to dream about it.

As the Perkins brothers jumped off the wagon, one rider aimed his horse toward David and attempted to yank the small hunting bag off his shoulder.

David refused to let go, and the boy on the horse jerked David backward and flung him into the mud. E. Z. reached to pull David toward the wagon in the nick of time to prevent the hind legs of the horse from crushing his brother.

E. Z. yelled at the boy, "Slow down, Jack, before you kill somebody!"

The boy only laughed and took out his whip to hit the horse to spur him on faster. E. Z. noticed that the boy's hat had a shiny silver band that glistened almost like glass in the sunlight.

As E. Z. helped his brother up and knocked cakes of mud off his back, David asked, "Do you know him?"

E. Z. said, "No."

"You called him 'Jack,'" David said.

E. Z. said, "I just called him 'Jack' because I didn't know his name. 'Jack' fits him."

E. Z. tried to make sense of the clamoring activity on the square to make sure no one else tried to run over them. People, horses, and cattle were coming and going on all four sides. A man playing a fiddle was surrounded by a small crowd that clapped along with the rhythm of his tune. Men shouted even when regular conversation would do.

As E. Z. studied the crowd of strangers, his neck tingled. He sensed a strange intuition that someone was watching him. Someone was talking about him. He stopped and ran his gaze almost in a circle around the square. But no one appeared to be looking back.

The wagon had stopped at a large, wooden building with a sign that read "Nashville Inn." Men sat on the porch whittling and spitting tobacco. A few of them stopped to stare at the family as they took time to scrape the mud from their shoes before entering the inn.

One man with long, stringy, black hair ran his knife back and forth on a whetstone to sharpen it. The man squinted at E. Z. when he spotted the hunting bag. His knife screeched on the whetstone as E. Z. passed. When E. Z. flinched in response, the man grinned. E. Z. convinced himself that one of those men must have been the one who was watching him.

The heavy entry door opened into a large common room on the first floor, where travelers took their meals and socialized. The inn smelled faintly like the smoke from the large stone fireplace at the end of the room. Smoke had soaked into the wooden ceiling, floors, and walls, darkening them all.

"It looks haunted," David said, squinting to peer into dark areas to see where they led. "Do we have to stay here?"

People seated around the tables appeared not to notice the darkness. Their loud talk and laughter echoed off the wood and made the crowded room seem brighter.

As Sarah worked out arrangements with the innkeeper, the boys were drawn to food being prepared for supper at the hearth. Chicken and beef turned on spits over the fire. Juices dripped down from the meat into the fire and spread their aroma with the heat. Whatever was cooking in the iron pots was the most appetizing food the boys had smelled since they had enjoyed their last meal at home.

As the boys stood at the hearth drooling over the pots, Sarah rushed over to pull them back. "We can't afford to eat here. I packed a few things for our supper."

A tall, gray-haired old man seated at the table next to the hearth with his daughter turned to listen to Sarah.

The man stood. "Madam, I couldn't help noticing your family when you came in. I would be honored if you and your boys would be my family's guests at supper." He introduced himself as "Captain Stark".

The "captain" title came from his service with General Washington in the Revolution. Still a soldier at heart, the old man wore a hunting shirt like the ones that soldiers in the Revolution used as uniforms.

Captain Stark chuckled, "You look skeptical, Madam. Let me show you the scar I got at the battle at Trenton." He tugged at his shirt to open it to prove his service. The captain was a jovial man who laughed through the stories he told to entertain people around him.

Captain Stark's daughter pushed his hand away to stop him. She introduced herself as "Mary Stewart" and begged Sarah and her family to join them. Mrs. Stewart was a small woman in simple frontier dress. She spoke so softly that her voice sounded like she was apologizing for taking the time of the person listening to her.

E. Z. was surprised that his mother accepted the invitation. She normally refused charity, but she rarely failed to assist anyone who needed her. Mrs. Stewart's voice was so timid Sarah must have assumed that Mrs. Stewart was asking for help.

E. Z. knew his mother well. She was letting down her guard. Her eyes showed a hint of fear for the first time. She had taken her children hundreds of miles from home. With little help or support, they would head into The Wilderness to start a new life. Now that the family was on the edge of the frontier at Nashville, E. Z.'s mother was doubting her decision.

The door to the outside opened, and Mary's husband, John Stewart, walked in with their son Isaiah. Isaiah was about a foot shorter than E. Z. Like his grandfather, Isaiah wore a hunting shirt, and his black hair was slicked back with cooking lard to look shiny.

As Isaiah followed his father across the common room, he stopped to hide behind chairs, appearing to be tracking an enemy soldier or Indian warrior.

"Stop that!" Mr. Stewart snapped. "You're drawing attention!" Mr. Stewart, dressed in a long, brown riding coat, looked so ordinary that most people would never notice him.

Isaiah's younger sister Hannah tagged along just behind. Her blond hair and round, angelic face stood her apart from the rest of her dark-haired family. Hannah giggled loudly at her brother's antics, egging him on.

The Stewart children joined the Perkins brothers at the fireplace and introduced themselves. Isaiah bragged that his grandfather had fought with General Washington in the Revolution and that he also wanted to become a soldier. "You probably guessed that by looking at me," he said as he made a show of making himself look stronger than he was.

Hannah rolled her eyes and sighed, "That's all he talks about."

David said, "I want to become a soldier, too. I want to build forts." David pulled out his drawing tablet to show his drawings but stashed it away quickly when no one showed any interest.

Hannah made her body appear limp as she pretended a fainting spell. "This long trip will take *forever* if all you talk about is soldiers," she said. "We will all die from boredom."

Hannah brushed the hair of the doll her grandfather had given her to keep her entertained. "Isaiah, can't you think of anything to make our trip more exciting?" Hannah was growing out of the doll phase of her life, and she did not yet know how to talk on the level of those older.

When none of the boys paid attention to Hannah, she made a sudden recovery from her faint. To their relief, she rushed off to join the women for more interesting talk. The boys could talk openly without worrying about frightening a young girl.

David motioned for the boys to follow him to the corner, away from most of the guests. He showed Isaiah the hunting bag.

"Where did you get it?" Isaiah asked.

"A boatman gave it to me. He said that we would need it," E. Z. interjected.

"Look! It's a soldier's. It's got blood stains on it. It must have been carried in battle," David said.

"Where will you put yours?" Isaiah asked.

"Where will I put what?" David asked.

"Your blood stains. It looks like the man who carries that bag is forced to mark it with his blood as he's dying." Isaiah attempted to joke as he put his hand across his throat and allowed his tongue to hang out of his mouth.

David did not respond. He looked at the stains and handed the bag to E. Z. to carry.

Isaiah bragged, "Look at my new knife. It's probably a soldier's, too. It's shaped like a small sword," and he pulled it out of a leather scabbard in his coat pocket to show E. Z. and David. It was unlike any knife they had seen back home. Rich engravings covered the handle.

A rough man, seated a few feet away at a table in the corner, jumped up when he saw the hunting bag and knife. A deep scar cut across the man's cheek. His left ear was missing. His dirty fingernails were long enough to be claws.

The man sneered at the children. "Ye'll use that where yo're headed. I hope a little blood won't take the shine off it for ye."

E. Z. was unsure whether the man was talking about the knife or the hunting bag. Isaiah's face lost its confidence. He turned to look toward his father, who had his back turned to the children.

"Do ye know where that knife has been?" the man asked.

"My Pa bought it from one of the peddlers on the street," Isaiah said.

"He did, did he? Maybe he did, and maybe he didn't," the rough man said. Then looking at the hunting bag, "Yore Pa got that at the same place, I reckon."

David answered, "My Pa is dead."

The man walked toward the children. Isaiah clutched his knife to prevent the man from taking it. E. Z. hung the hunting bag strap across his own shoulder and stepped in front of David.

The man pointed his finger. "Ye know what the Indians do to chil'lun yore size?" He leaned down close. "Them Indians got some big pots over their fires. There'll be a few pots you'll fit in, I reckon. Chil'lun soup is a fav-o-rite of the Indians." He turned toward the door, bursting out laughing, followed by a fit of coughing as he walked outside.

As the man walked out, E. Z. noticed the bright cloth coat the man was wearing. It did not look like the type of coat a man who acted like that would wear. It also looked too small for him, as if the man were wearing someone else's coat.

"Do you know who that man was?" E. Z. asked.

Isaiah answered, "No. He was sitting over there in the corner when we got here about noon. He stared at me and seemed to be listening to every word we said. I was afraid that if he caught me looking back at him, I would have had to fight him off." Isaiah held out his arm to flex a small muscle. "I didn't want to hurt him."

E. Z. asked, "Where are you going that you will need the knife?"

"Down the Natchez Trace," Isaiah said.

"So are we," David added.

"I wonder why that man said we will need the knife," Isaiah asked. "The innkeeper told us the area we're headed is called 'The Wilderness.' Is it dangerous?"

"Boatmen told me stories about bandits and Indians on the road. One said that the road so dangerous that some call it 'The Devil's Backbone,'" E. Z. said.

Isaiah looked puzzled. "'The Devil's Backbone'? What kind of name is that?"

E. Z. said, "They said it's a mysterious place. Strange things happen to people on the road. I don't know whether all the stories are true, but I think the bandits are real."

Isaiah said, "That man was real enough. Did you notice that his left ear was missing? Pa says that when a man does something bad in a town, the others run him out. Before they do, though, they brand him or cut off a piece to mark him so that people in the next town he goes to know to watch him."

E. Z. thought of the wild-eyed boatman's missing thumb. What crime was bad enough to deserve that punishment?

The boys continued to speculate about the man who had just left. David was certain that he could be a Spanish spy. Isaiah suggested that he might be a pirate stranded on land. The boys finally reached agreement that the man was a land pirate, robber, or a bandit who rode the Natchez Trace.

E. Z. revealed his worry, "One of the boatmen told me that sometimes bandits pick out their victims at the inns along the Natchez Trace. Then they follow them down the road and attack them when the victims don't suspect there is any danger. Bandits might rob them for no more than a shiny new knife."

The children looked at the knife that Isaiah held in a hand that was now trembling. He did not seem as proud of his new treasure. Isaiah held the knife up to his face like a pet and talked to it, "I guess I had better sharpen you. You will earn your keep on the mysterious Natchez Trace."

E. Z. scolded David, "You shouldn't have told the bandit that our father is dead."

"But he is," David said.

E. Z. gave David that "older brother" look that David hated. "If we are going into a dangerous area, we can't tell everybody our business. They will take advantage of us if they think we can't defend ourselves."

"How long has your Pa been dead?" Isaiah asked.

"About five years," E. Z. said. "He died from fever when David was small."

"You don't have any men in your party?" Isaiah asked.

E. Z. shook his head. "No. We have been on our own since Pa died. Our family is all gone. Ma said David and I would wind up working for somebody else our whole life if we stayed at home. She heard we can get rich on the frontier."

"I wish we were traveling together. We could gang up on whatever tries to attack us," Isaiah said as he acted out a wrestling hold and knocked over a couple chairs.

Sarah's sudden presence surprised them. "Isaiah, I am Ezekiel and David's mother, "Sarah Perkins". I met your mother." Sarah licked her hand and rubbed David's head to flatten his cowlick. "We have been invited to join Isaiah's family for supper as their guests. I told his family about our plans to travel down the Natchez Trace."

E. Z. wanted to tell his mother about the man they suspected to be a bandit. But boatmen had warned that bandits would kill anyone who knew their true identities. He and David now added up to the one man of the family, and it was their job to protect their mother from bandits.

After the children were seated on the long wooden benches at the table, servants brought pots from the hearth. The children held up their plates as servants dipped out savory broth, beef, and vegetables onto the plates and added a hot cornmeal bread.

Isaiah raised a spoonful of broth. "Mmm. Chil'lun soup." He and Hannah laughed, but E. Z. did not appreciate the joke. He was too hungry.

Sarah interrupted, "The Stewarts were just telling me that it is common for families to meet in Nashville and form traveling parties before setting out down the road. It seems that the Natchez Trace may be more dangerous than I was told. Your boatman was right about bandits. There will be safety in numbers if we travel together. The Stewarts have invited us to travel with them."

The children watched each other and communicated without talking. E. Z. sought assurance that Isaiah would not reveal their secret of the bandit. Isaiah half nodded. The new friends were happy to be traveling together. There would be safety in their numbers too.

"We moved into town back home after my husband died. My sons have not had much experience in the woods," Sarah told Mary.

"Isaiah hasn't either. I am afraid he will not be able to teach your sons anything about the outdoors," Mary added.

E. Z. turned away in embarrassment that his mother had revealed his lack of frontier skills. The bandit stared back through a window pane. E. Z. caught his gaze and gulped.

CHAPTER THREE

Chosen

———

The bandit held up a long, gold object that glistened with the reflection of candles from inside. E. Z. had never seen anything like it. The bandit motioned his head for E. Z. to follow him. E. Z. excused himself from the table to visit the privy outdoors.

By the time E. Z. walked out to the porch, the bandit had disappeared. The sun had set, and the streets were practically empty. A heavy fog had descended on the town. Even though a man was lighting torch lamps along the streets, it was still difficult to see who might be standing in the shadows.

E. Z. stepped out into the street and walked behind the inn. As he tried to look through the fog to see where the bandit had gone, packs of rats ran from the corn crib by the stables and scurried around his feet. The largest rat bit at his boots and chirped to encourage the others to join him. E. Z. kicked them away to keep them from running up his britches. The largest ones hissed back in fury.

"Care killed the cat!" the bandit snarled from behind E. Z.

E. Z. jumped in surprise.

"I knew ye would have to know what I was holdin' up." The bandit walked faster toward E. Z. "Come closer, and I'll tell ye all about it." Pointing to the rats, he added, "Careful to mind my little friends."

E. Z. ran away from the bandit and rats towards the side of the inn.

The bandit walked faster. "Ye've been chosen, my young friend. And thar's nothin' ye can do about it now!"

The bandit could not match E. Z.'s speed, and he disappeared into the fog as E. Z. raced away. E. Z. backed onto the side porch to hide, bumping boxes of roosters the innkeeper kept for gambling. The chickens had already roosted for the night, but they let out a loud gaggle that should have drawn the bandit's attention. E. Z. stood sideways behind the porch post and held his breath to make himself even thinner to hide.

E. Z. waited for what seemed to be an eternity as the fog grew heavier. Then he spotted a man who wore a coat and hat that looked like the ones worn by the bandit. E. Z. followed the man toward the stables behind the inn. The man stopped at the stables door and looked up and down the street.

The man entered the stables, leaving the door slightly open, seeming to invite E. Z. inside.

E. Z. did not take the bait. He waited.

After a few minutes when the man had not come out, E. Z. walked out to the street to try to peer inside the stables door. He saw only darkness.

E. Z. wheeled around to return to the inn and ran right into a group of men standing behind him.

The men were dressed odd for Nashville. They were Indians.

The tall Indian in front wore a turban on his head, calico shirt, and leather leggings. Earrings dangled from his ears. A silver gorget hung around his neck. The others were dressed the same. They watched the man in front for direction.

E. Z. looked for spears or arrows. He was relieved to see none. Then he spotted sharp hatchets that hung on belts on the Indians' waists.

The Indian men walked around E. Z. in a semi-circle. He felt trapped, but then they spread out and stood between him and the stables.

The Indian leader in front gave E. Z. a stern stare. He pointed toward the stables where the man had entered and said, "Bad man! You go!"

E. Z. did not hesitate. He ran as fast as he could back to the inn and burst through the door. Everyone looked at E. Z. as if he had been the bandit.

Sarah scowled at E. Z. as he took his place at the table, while trying not to draw more attention to himself.

E. Z. wanted to tell David and Isaiah what he had seen, but it would have to wait until after supper. Isaiah had asked Captain Stark to talk about the war, and the captain went on and on about the Battle of Trenton. Isaiah's face beamed as his grandfather talked about outwitting the British. David hung on every word, occasionally stopping the action to ask how they had built their cabins or forts.

E. Z. interrupted, "Did you ever fight any Indians, Captain Stark?"

Captain Stark had to admit that he had not and quickly went back to his fights with the British.

"If you had to fight Indians, what would you use?" E. Z. interrupted again.

"Ezekiel," Sarah said, "It is not polite to interrupt your elders."

"No, Madam. That is alright," the captain said. "Why do you ask, boy?"

"Some of the boatmen told me that we might see Creek or Shawnee Indians on the Natchez Trace and that they might try to kill us." E. Z. paused and then excitedly blurted out, "There might be Indians here in Nashville!"

Captain Stark laughed and called over the innkeeper. "Young Ezekiel here is worried that Creek and Shawnee Indians have stolen into Nashville. What do you suggest we do?"

The innkeeper scratched his head, pretending to be deep in thought. "Well, if that be the case, the night watchman has fallen asleep. We need to alert him to sound an alarm for the militia. They will send for General Jackson. He's in command of the defense, and he will know what to do."

The innkeeper leaned down and warned, "But you do not want to rouse the general on a false alarm. His anger is a matter of legend around here."

E. Z. was not intimidated. "I think I saw some Indians when I went outside to the privy." He described the gorgets, the turbans, and earrings—what he could recall.

"Were their faces painted?" the innkeeper asked.

"Painted?"

"Indians paint their faces for war with a red ochre. It makes their appearance more frightening to their enemies. And Indians do not usually loiter around town before attacking. You would have heard war whoops."

"What would those sound like?"

"The older settlers described them as the sound of a thousand devils. Warriors make those sounds to scare their victims into running."

"No, Sir. I didn't hear any screams. They just talked to me."

"*Talked* to you? What did they say?"

"They told me... to go back inside."

The innkeeper smiled, "Well, young Ezekiel, I will let you in on a secret." He lowered his head to the children and whispered, "Nashville does have Indians."

The children's mouths opened. David immediately turned to look out the window.

"They are Chickasaw Indians. Their nation is just south and west of Nashville, and they come into town to trade with us. The Chickasaws have always been our friends. In fact, it was Chickasaw Chief Piominko who first allowed us to live here. If the Creek or Shawnee plan an attack, the Chickasaws are the first to tell us. Now, did the Indians you saw warn you that you were going to be attacked?"

Of course, in a sense they had, but E. Z. feared that if he told the adults about the bandit, it would put his family in danger. He tried to change the subject. "Do Creek Indians boil children in pots?"

The innkeeper's belly shook as he laughed. In Nashville, parents often told their children bedtime stories about vicious witches, ghosts, or Indian warriors. The stories kept the children from wandering too far outside in the dark where real dangers might lurk.

The innkeeper said, "Well, they don't boil *good* children in pots," and he continued laughing as he walked away.

Now the adults would not believe anything E. Z. said about the bandit. Maybe that is why the bandit had told him about boiling pots.

The innkeeper's answer did not make E. Z. feel any better sleeping at the inn. In the middle of summer, it was too hot to sleep inside. Most travelers slept on the porches on bedrolls they carried with them. Children slept on pallets made from blankets.

There would be some safety in numbers but sleeping outside would expose the boys to the bandit and Indians.

The boys agreed that they would share a pallet on the floor. They promised that they would each take a turn keeping watch while the others slept.

E. Z. soon discovered that he was the only one who could stay awake. The town watchman came around once an hour to announce the time and weather, but he barely could be heard over the loud snoring.

A few minutes after the town watchman announced, "three o' the clock," E. Z. noticed movement out toward the stables. He tried to wake David and Isaiah without waking anyone else. They were too deep in sleep. E. Z. was on his own.

Through the fog, E. Z. saw the figure of a man wearing what looked like the bandit's hat ride a horse to the stables door as he pulled along a second horse with a rope. E. Z. assumed the man was the bandit they had seen earlier. But then, the man wearing the bandit's hat dragged a lifeless body from the stables, put it across the back of the second horse, tied the body to the horse, and began to lead the horse away from town. The body was dressed in the coat that the bandit had been wearing.

Both men could not be the bandit. Maybe E. Z. had followed the wrong man to the stables.

A second rider appeared and rode alongside the body tied to the horse for a distance. Suddenly, the second rider broke away and turned toward the inn. Did he know that E. Z. had seen him?

A silver band on the rider's hat reflected light from the street torches, cutting through the fog. It appeared to be the same hat he had seen 'Jack' wearing earlier in the day. E. Z. raised his head to get a better look. Jack saw him. Jack jerked his horse back toward the porch.

E. Z. laid down his head and pretended to close his eyes. He kept them open just enough to see. He tried holding his breath, but he failed. He was too scared.

Jack walked the horse slowly by the porch twice. When Jack paused to stare at E. Z., E. Z. shut his eyes. Jack's whip cracked as he struck his horse and rode off to join the other rider and what appeared to be a dead man tied to a horse.

CHAPTER FOUR

The Mysterious Mr. Burton

"I saw the bandit again," E. Z. said to wake up the boys as the sun began to rise. "I think he killed a man in the stables. I saw him tie a body to a horse and they rode off."

"You saw a body?" David jolted up and wiped the morning sleep from his eyes. "That could have been you. I'm glad you didn't go in the stables last night."

Other guests began stirring on the porch and going inside to pour water into bowls to wash their hands and faces for breakfast.

Isaiah was awake and curious. "You said 'they.' Was there more than one bandit?"

"Jack, the fella that almost ran over David today, was with him. I recognized the silver band on his hat."

"Why didn't you wake me?" Isaiah asked. "There were three of us. We had them outnumbered."

"I tried," E. Z. said, adding, "You were sleeping as sound as a baby," to challenge Isaiah's brags of bravery.

"Where did they go?" David asked as he looked down the street to see if they were still around.

E. Z. said, "Out in the direction of the Natchez Trace. They know that I saw them. They'll be waiting for us out there somewhere. We have to tell someone."

The boys hurried inside only to wait as the adults finished their meal. At large meals, children ate last from whatever food was left over when the adults finished. The wait gave E. Z. time to survey the room to decide whether there was any adult he could tell.

E. Z. wanted to tell his mother, but he also wanted to protect her. He would expect Captain Stark to launch into more battle stories, and he did not expect the bandit to show up with an army. The innkeeper did not take E. Z. seriously after his question about boiling pots. Isaiah's father John was the last hope. But E. Z. was not sure. John Stewart had said little at dinner the night before. He seemed troubled already.

"Isaiah, we need to tell your father," E. Z. said.

Isaiah dropped his head. "I wish we could, but we can't.

"Why not?" David asked.

"David!" E. Z. rapped David on the head. It was obvious Isaiah wanted to say more but chose not to.

E. Z. gave up on finding help. "I can't think of anybody else. It'll be up to us. We'll just have to keep a sharp eye."

Sarah interrupted, "Are you boys keeping secrets? You look like you are plotting something dastardly. Come on over to the table. The men are almost finished, and I want to you to meet someone who wants to join our party down the Natchez Trace."

Sarah licked her hand to wet down David's cowlick and straighten his hair. Then she spat into a small handkerchief and rubbed David's face to wipe off any dirt. David grimaced. But he had learned it did no good to object when his mother wanted him to make a good impression on a stranger.

The boys surveyed the room to see who had not slept on the porch. A dark-haired, middle-aged man dressed in fine clothes was seated at the end of the Stewarts' table. Small scars on his face suggested that he had survived challenges in his life.

Sarah said, "We were talking about how the three of us were traveling alone with the Stewart family, and he offered to come along. We will be safer if we have another man with us for protection."

The man looked up from the last of the biscuits, butter, and molasses on his plate. "Well, good morning. My name is 'Joshua Burton'. Your mothers may want you to call me 'Mr. Burton,' but I am fine with 'Joshua.'"

"Are you going down the Natchez Trace, Mr. Joshua?" David asked.

"If you will permit me to join you. I have some business in the Mississippi Territory that I hope will improve my life. I was waiting for the right group to begin the journey."

Mr. Burton must have bought some of the Paris, France clothes from one of the street vendors. They were the fanciest E. Z. had ever seen. But he also noticed that Mr. Burton's boots were not fancy. That was strange. Men usually put more thought into the style of their boots than coats.

Mr. Burton wiped his hands on a napkin. He stood and shook the hand of each boy and nodded at Hannah who was joining the boys for breakfast.

"I can see that we will be great friends by the time our journey has ended," Mr. Burton said.

"Are you any good with a gun, Mr. Burton?" E. Z. asked.

"I can take care of myself," Mr. Burton answered with a glance toward Sarah.

"Can you protect the rest of us, too?" E. Z. added.

Mr. Burton laughed. "Are you expecting trouble, Ezekiel?"

E. Z. did not laugh. "That's why we are traveling together isn't it? We might meet Creek or Shawnee warriors…. or bandits."

Mr. Burton squinted. "Bandits? Why, I suppose we could meet bandits on the Natchez Trace… What have you heard about them?"

E. Z. said, "Some of the boatmen told me that bandits hide in caves and in canebrakes along the road. Then, when travelers least suspect it, bandits rush out and rob the travelers and kill them. They said that a bandit is especially likely to kill anyone who tells who the bandit is."

Mr. Burton said, "Then it is a good thing we are traveling in a group. I will be sure to keep my pistols on the ready."

E. Z. did not know whether he could trust Mr. Burton enough just yet to tell him about Jack or the bandit that E. Z. had followed to the stables. He would wait to see whether the gentleman dressed in fancy clothes knew anything about pistols.

"Was your father in the army, Ezekiel?" Mr. Burton asked.

"Yes....Yes, Sir."

"I noticed your hunting bag. I have seen soldiers on the Natchez Trace carry those. Mind if I have a look at it?"

Mr. Burton did not wait for an answer before reaching toward it. E. Z. stepped back, out of Mr. Burton's reach. E. Z. did not know why. It was instinct.

Sarah noticed that the conversation was not going as she had hoped. "Now, you boys don't trouble Mr. Burton too much. You need to go on and get some breakfast. I hear that we will be leaving by late morning now that we have enough in our party to fill a wagon."

She apologized to Mr. Burton, "My boys seem to have quite an imagination. I am sorry if they were impolite."

"No need to apologize," he said with a smile. "I was their age once. We will get along fine."

Sarah took the boys aside. "You need to be more polite to the people we meet. We need all the friends we can get out here."

"I don't trust him," E. Z. said.

"And, why not? He is a gentleman," Sarah said. "You could learn a great deal from Mr. Burton about how a man should act in this area."

"There's just something about him that doesn't seem right. We don't know anything about him."

"I am sure that we will get to know everyone in our party in no time."

Sarah lightened the tone of her voice as she usually did when she was trying to change E. Z.'s mood. "I have a surprise. We put our money together to hire a wagon and buy a separate horse to help carry supplies. It was Captain Stark's idea. He said that they used packhorses when he was in the army."

Sarah's surprise did not work. E. Z. was even more concerned. "A horse? Do we have enough money to buy a horse?"

"Together, we all do. I used some of the money I saved for land to pay our part. When we get to the territory, we can sell the horse." Sarah stepped over close to E. Z.'s ear and whispered, "The rest I have sewn in my dress. If we see any of your bandits, I won't make it easy for them to find it. Mary heard that travelers often hide their money in their clothes. She is doing the same. Now hurry and get some breakfast. Don't keep us waiting."

The boys ate little before running to the long front porch to be first to see the hired wagon and the new horse. Hannah refused to stay behind and tagged along. Each boy gave his own prediction of what kind of horse it would be. When a man rode an Appaloosa up to the porch and asked for Captain Stark, the boys were crestfallen.

"That can't be the horse," Isaiah said. "It's got spots!"

Captain Stark stepped out to the porch to see the horse. "Fine. Fine. She will do fine." He clapped his hands together in excitement.

Isaiah said, "That horse won't win any races. She already sags and we haven't put anything on her yet."

Captain Stark overheard and laughed, "We don't want a racehorse. It wouldn't get very far. These Appaloosas are Chickasaw horses. They are bred to carry loads. Slow and steady. And reliable. That's what we need."

E. Z. was still disappointed. His family had never had money to buy a horse, and this horse was not the one he had imagined. "At least we don't have to worry about a bandit stealing our horse. Nobody but us would want it."

"Quiet!" Hannah rushed over toward the horse. "She will hear you. Horses know when you are talking about them." Hannah began to rub the horse's head. She put her mouth close to the ear of the horse. "Don't mind anything the boys say. All they think about are soldiers, and bandits, and Indians."

"And *good-looking* horses," Isaiah added to needle his sister.

Hannah paid her brother no attention. She asked the man, "What is her name?"

The man said, "Esther. She is gentle. Give her plenty of oats or corn and she'll work hard for you."

Hannah put her head against Esther's. "Esther. We are going to be good friends, since the boys won't let me be theirs."

Six oxen with horns, yoked in two rows, pulled a large blue wagon up to the inn. The wagon had high wooden sides to carry both people and cargo. And it sagged in the middle.

A loud "whoa" boomed from the front of the wagon and echoed off the building across the street.

E. Z. asked, "Is that wagon sagging in the middle on purpose?"

Captain Stark answered, "That puts the weight low to the ground. It keeps it from tipping over on a steep bank." And, to rile up Isaiah, the captain added with a chuckle, "Just like Esther."

Isaiah was not impressed. "The Indians will be too busy laughing at us to kill us."

The wagon driver looked as tough as the oxen. His face was leathered from years outdoors. His black hair under his floppy, wide-brimmed hat had never seen a comb. And he spat constantly. He was chewing tobacco. "Don't get downwind, boy," is all he would tell E. Z. about it.

A dog popped its head up over the top of the wagon. After letting out a couple quick barks, it jumped to the ground and began sniffing the children's legs and shoes.

Hannah squealed and jumped back.

"He's not tryin' to bite you," the driver said. "That's how he's gettin' to know who you are. His name's 'Major' — I would've called him 'General,' but he's only second-in-command. I didn't want to give him any notion that he's in charge of this operation. Dogs understand more than you think."

Major trotted over to each boy, placing his head close to his hand, as if begging to be petted. Each welcomed the chance to become Major's friend. When Isaiah reached out, the dog sniffed Isaiah's new knife hanging in a scabbard from his belt. Major immediately backed up, the small hair on his back stood up, and he started barking.

"Major! Get up here!" the driver commanded. The dog obeyed and jumped up on the driver's bench. "He's never done that before. Thar's somethin' about that knife he don't like. You ain't killed any bears with it have you?"

Isaiah's eyes widened. "I don't know what has been killed with it. I just got it."

The driver said, "You might go inside and stick it in the fire for a bit. See if it'll burn off whatever it's carryin' around. If it's a strong knife, the fire won't hurt it. Might make it stronger. Kind'a like this trip we're fixin' to take. It'll make y'all stronger, but you may think yo're in the fire from time to time."

E. Z. looked at the others, wondering what kind of "fire" they would be getting into and whether it would be in pots over a fire as the bandit had told them.

The driver spat. Then he studied each of the children like a captain inspecting his troops. He added, "I reckon y'all are pretty tough. We'll soon find out."

As Isaiah ran inside to purify his knife in the fire, he passed Sarah and the Stewarts, who were coming out to see the wagon. The driver introduced himself as "Thaddeus Johnson." He had traveled the Natchez Trace several times, he said. E. Z. was surprised that Mr. Johnson had survived the bandits and Indians on that many trips. He thought Mr. Johnson must be as tough as he looked.

Mr. Johnson told the women that there would be few places to buy food once they left the settled areas. "Stock up on flour, salted pork, jerky, sugar, and roasted corn. If thar's too much rain to build a fire to cook one night, you can mix roasted cornmeal with water and sugar and drink it. It'll keep you goin' fine 'til the next supper."

David pointed to clay jugs that Mr. Johnson carried in his wagon. "Is that your corn and sugar drink, Mr. Johnson?"

"Yep. Liquid corn. But it ain't for children. Just wagon drivers," he said. He never offered to share it.

As soon as Mr. Johnson had loaded supplies on the wagon, everyone prepared to crowd in. After a brief debate, the adults finally agreed that Captain Stark should have the honor of riding Esther. But he preferred to ride in the wagon and keep everyone entertained with his stories.

Mr. Burton stepped forward and said that if he rode Esther, it would give the horse time to get to know him.

The party had invested their money in her. He would be able to keep her from running off on the Natchez Trace. That was a common problem with new horses, he said. Esther let out a long, disapproving neigh when Mr. Burton sat on her.

Hannah said, "They should have let Esther choose who would ride her. She would have picked me."

Once everyone was seated, Mr. Johnson snapped the reins, spat more tobacco juice, and began singing a song to the two lead oxen in front. "Now get along Jim, get along Ole' Henry...." and the wagon began to move.

CHAPTER FIVE

The Escape

"**W**hat's around the next hill? Have you seen any Indians yet? Look! Is that the barrel of a bandit's pistol?" the boys kept shouting to Mr. Johnson from the back of the wagon.

Mr. Johnson grew impatient with each answer he shouted back. When he stopped responding, it became obvious that he was pretending that he could not hear. The boys would not give up.

Mr. Johnson finally stopped the wagon and invited E. Z. and Isaiah to ride beside him on the springboard driver's bench. E. Z. insisted that David join them. The flat, wooden board was hard, but the metal spring beneath the seat absorbed some of the shock of the rough road.

Major was usually the only sidekick allowed to sit by the driver. At first, Major was reluctant to abandon his post on the driver's seat, but when the boys began to pet him, he moved down to the buckboard floor. The dog seemed satisfied having the boys' company. But the lower position did not stop him from jumping up to bark at squirrels and rabbits they passed.

"We still have a ways to go before we run out of the settled areas," Mr. Johnson told them. "Facts of the matter, I decided to take the route through Franklin whar the road is better, and whar the women can buy more food before we go out into The Wilderness."

"There's another road?" Isaiah asked.

"Thar's a couple more roads we could've taken out of Nashville toward Natchez, but they ain't as good as this 'un. This here's the new wagon highway. During the summer when it's dry, except after a heavy rain like that gulley washer in Nashville yesterday, the roadbed is real firm and wagon wheels roll faster.

"What are the other roads like?" David asked.

"If we had taken the one past Harding's, I could've showed you whar Creek Indians killed the Dunham family. They still use the house as an inn—of course, they washed off all the blood."

E. Z. was relieved but a little disappointed to miss the scene of an Indian attack. So far, at least, they had met a steady stream of travelers in wagons and buggies and on horseback. E. Z. did not sense that they were getting closer to The Wilderness or to the mysterious part of the Natchez Trace.

"Halloo!" shouted a rider from the distance.

Mr. Johnson squinted. "Ah, that would be Swaney, the post rider. Now, that feller could answer lots'a yore questions. He rides the whole road all the way to Natchez and back twice a month carryin' the mail."

Mr. Swaney was young. Like Mr. Johnson, the post rider wore a wide-brimmed hat and riding coat with a wide collar that kept him dry in the rain. His horse was loaded down with deerskin mail bags. E. Z. compared them to the one the boatman had given him. They were similar. But E. Z.'s was too small to be an official mail bag.

"Any news ahead, Swaney?" Mr. Johnson yelled.

"Rangers lookin' fer a bandit who robbed an' killed a rider at Swan Creek 'bout a week ago. Keep alert!" Mr. Swaney shouted as he passed.

"Where is Swan Creek?" E. Z. asked.

"A couple days' ride ahead. Lots'a travelers been killed thar. Bandits hide in caves above the creek," Mr. Johnson answered. "Facts of the matter, after some men was killed by robbers at Swan Creek a few years back, the government started building stations along the road to provide shelter for families like yours. You can be thankful for that. Of course, sometimes sleepin' inside those inns is more dangerous than sleepin' outside and takin' yore chances. That's what lots'a folks do."

Mr. Johnson pulled the wagon to the side of the road and stopped. He turned to announce, "Now, folks, thar's a good spring here. Fill yore canteens with fresh water… and take care of whatever else you need to do."

As E. Z. jumped off the wagon, he saw movement from the corner of his eye. Something large with black fur crossed the road ahead. He could not be sure. Could it have been one of the hairy creatures the boatman warned him about? Major should have been barking at it, but he was busy chasing a squirrel. E. Z. did not want the adults laughing at him again as they had when he suggested the Creek Indians might boil him. He would wait to see if they saw it again.

The families climbed down out of the wagon. It was a shady spot. As Mr. Johnson fed and watered the oxen, Sarah and Mary pulled out small packages of biscuits and pork left over from breakfast. It was not much, but it would serve as dinner for the children.

Hannah pulled grass to feed Esther. Occasionally, the horse put her head next to Hannah's as if to thank her for the attention.

E. Z. had wanted to explore the woods near the spring, but he did not want to encounter the creature, whatever it was. He suggested that the boys eat their noon dinner near the wagon.

Between bites, the boys discussed the bandits ahead. They began to plot how they would fight back in self-defense if they were attacked. Mr. Johnson kept a gun, and Mr. Burton had one too.

But Isaiah did not respond to any questions about whether his father was armed. He changed the subject and bragged, "Mr. Johnson asked if I had killed a bear with the knife. I'll have to tell you boys about my bear-killing adventures sometime."

"We have time now," David said innocently, as if he did not understand that Isaiah was joking.

"I'll save those stories for down the road when we see our first bear," Isaiah said.

Mr. Burton was in the woods for so long that Sarah began asking whether he had gotten lost. "Ezekiel, do you think one of the bandits you talked about got Mr. Burton?"

The bushes behind Sarah rustled. E. Z. thought of the hairy creature.

"You would have heard shots first," Mr. Burton said from behind her as he appeared from the woods and startled her. He said that he had gone searching for some red root as medicine for his joints and had trouble finding his way back. He also must not have found any red root, because he had none with him.

Mr. Johnson was starting to become cantankerous. He told Mr. Burton that if he took that long again at a stop, he would leave him behind, even if they were in the heart of Indian country. Mr. Burton's face flashed red in sudden anger, but just as quickly, he stopped and smiled and said, "I understand."

Mr. Stewart came out of the woods behind Mr. Burton. Mr. Johnson had not seen him, or he would have heard the same strong words.

At Mr. Johnson's signal, Major began barking and circling everyone to move them back toward the wagon, as if herding sheep. E. Z., David, and Isaiah took their seat next to Mr. Johnson as the wagon pulled away.

The boys discussed the farms along the road. Occasionally, a man they assumed to be the farm owner tipped his hat at their passing wagon. David bombarded E. Z. with questions about whether their farm would look the same. Would theirs have a sturdy house, stables, corn crib, and fields fenced with rails?

"It won't look like that for a long time. We'll have to clear the land and build everything," E. Z. said.

David paid more attention and began to draw a picture of where everything should be built on their farm.

E. Z. pointed to the enslaved black people working in the fields. "That's the work we'll be doing on our own farm after we're finished building."

David asked, "How much are the field workers paid?"

Mr. Johnson explained slavery, which he hated. He said that sometimes he met runaway slaves on the Natchez Trace. Other times, he met bandits who had kidnapped slaves and took them down the road to Natchez to sell them in the slave markets. They would never see their families again.

"Ma said she is moving us to the frontier so that we don't have to become slaves back home working for somebody else," E. Z. said.

"It ain't the same slavery," Mr. Johnson said.

David asked, "If E. Z. and I work as slaves on our farm, will we be kidnapped too?"

Mr. Johnson said, "You only have to worry about bein' a slave if yo're a sailor. The British are capturin' our sailors and makin' 'em slaves on thar ships. But if they live long enough, they'll be given wages and freedom. The farmhands in these fields will work as slaves their whole lives."

"The British had better not try to take me to work on a ship," Isaiah said. "I'll swim back and then we'll fight the Revolution all over again."

As the wagon came to the Harpeth River, E. Z. started to challenge Isaiah to a swimming contest across the river. Mr. Johnson diverted their attention by pointing to the town of Franklin just above the water. The boys were surprised that the town looked about as large as Nashville. The wagon circled around the hill until it came to a shallow area to ford the stream.

Mr. Johnson pulled the wagon to the front of White's Tavern near the river. It was a two-story, wooden building with large fireplaces in the center. Its porches were not as large as the ones at the Nashville Inn, but the boys planned to crowd onto them for the evening.

Mr. Burton followed on Esther, leaving her at the stables behind the inn. Hannah rushed out to take her some oats and to pet her.

The boys ran down the streets to explore the town. They found a large crowd gathered around the Court House in the center of the Public Square. With E. Z. in the lead, the boys pushed their way into the back of the room and saw that a trial was in progress. Spectators said it was the talk of the town.

Three judges were seated at the head table. One banged his gavel to silence the crowd.

A prisoner was charged with killing a traveler on the Natchez Trace. The prosecutor said that the man had met a traveler at an inn and asked to ride with him down the Natchez Trace for protection. The man had pretended to be a friend, but his whole intent was to wait until they were alone on the road. Then, he said, the prisoner had robbed and killed the traveler.

The boys stood on their toes hoping to see the face of the bandit. They had never seen a murderer. Surprisingly, the bandit did not look sinister. He could have been anyone they had met in Nashville at the inn.

E. Z. whispered, "We don't know anything about Mr. Burton. He just showed up at the inn."

"He has acted a little strange," Isaiah agreed. "Where did he go when we stopped for water?"

"Maybe we need to ask him more questions," E. Z. said. "Let's talk with him after supper tonight and see if we can get some information ………."

Gunshots fired outside the door. The deputy guarding the prisoner ran out the door to find out who was shooting. The prisoner saw his opportunity and bolted to a window on the opposite side of the room and jumped out.

"He's running away! Get him!," the judges shouted. There was a commotion in the front of the courtroom, but it was too crowded for the boys to see what was happening. The excited crowd ran out of the Court House, pushing the boys outdoors in the flow of the wave.

Townspeople outside also were excited. Men shouted that the prisoner had escaped. They said that two of the prisoner's friends wearing masks had ridden their horses up to the Court House and started firing their guns.

It had been a trick. As the gang had planned, the deputy ran to see who was shooting, leaving the prisoner unguarded. The prisoner's friends had ridden around to the opposite side of the building and were waiting for him. All three rode off in the direction of the Natchez Trace.

A deputy rang a bell on a post to sound an alarm as it seemed the whole town was suddenly in a stir. People rushed out of buildings onto the street.

In the confusion of people running in all directions, someone behind E. Z. tried to pull the hunting bag off his shoulder. He held on to it as tight as David had on the Nashville Public Square. E. Z. felt a sharp object prodding his back. As he started to turn to see who was pulling at the bag, the man shoved him into the people in front, and then ran back into the crowd behind. E. Z. studied the faces behind him, but he did not see anyone he recognized.

The sheriff appeared and began conscripting town citizens to ride after the prisoner. He shouted that the prisoner and his friend must be part of a larger gang on the Natchez Trace. He needed his own posse to fight them.

"Did you see the man who tried to steal the bag?" E. Z. asked Isaiah.

"Someone tried to steal the bag? No, there were too many people between us. I didn't see anybody," Isaiah said. Then attempting to stand taller, he added, "You should have yelled for me. I would have tackled him and held him until the sheriff came to arrest him."

The boys hurried back to White's Tavern to tell the adults what happened. Talk of the escape would keep the guests entertained the whole evening. Most of the men at the inn bragged that if they had been at the Court House, the prisoner would not have escaped. E. Z. noticed that none of the braggarts offered to leave the safety of the inn to join the sheriff's posse.

E. Z. searched for Mr. Burton at the inn. He wondered whether Mr. Burton could have been one of the masked men who had rescued the prisoner.

After the boys ate an early supper, they joined the men on the porch. Isaiah pretended that he had been deputized to look for Mr. Burton. E. Z. and David watched as Isaiah ran behind trees, scouting the area around the inn to keep watch for him.

To E. Z.'s surprise, Mr. Burton walked onto the porch and found a chair. He placed a tin cup of water down beside him. Small streams of sweat ran down Mr. Burton's face. He looked as if he had been working hard. The boys pulled up a bench near to him as planned.

"Have you ever been in Franklin before, Mr. Burton?" E. Z. started his questioning.

"My business has brought me this way a few times," Mr. Burton admitted as he wiped his forehead. "Why do you ask?"

"Just wondering if it was common for prisoners to run away from their trials. We were at the Court House today when a prisoner escaped." E. Z. said.

"Escaped? Well, it is a good thing you boys did not get in his way. You might not be around to talk with me tonight," Mr. Burton said. Then after sipping some cold water from his cup, he attempted some humor. "You never want to stand in the way of stampeding cattle or escaping prisoners. Neither will give any thought to who they hurt."

"Do bandits care who they hurt?" E. Z. asked, watching carefully to see how Mr. Burton responded.

"If they did, they wouldn't be bandits, now would they?" Mr. Burton answered without showing any emotion.

Isaiah pressed him, "What would make someone not care about who they hurt?"

Mr. Burton hesitated before answering. "I once heard of a man who was wrongly accused of theft. He was an innocent, law-abiding man. But he was found guilty of a crime that he did not commit, and the whole town turned on him. They did something to mark him as a thief. Put a brand to him or cut off a piece of his ear. It made him bitter against his neighbors." He took a pause to drink from the tin cup and stared into the distance before continuing.

"He gave in to revenge. It changed him. And to punish his accusers, he became the villain he was accused of being. Then he raised sons to help him carry out his revenge." He paused again in thought. "I suppose men become bandits for any number of reasons."

"What kinds of things did he do for revenge?" E. Z. asked.

"Most bandits in this area rely on their knives. He would take his knife and..." Mr. Burton hesitated when he saw that David had more than the usual fear in his eyes. "There was not much he wouldn't do."

As E. Z. prepared to press Mr. Burton for all the gruesome details, the bell sounded the alarm again on the Public Square. Panicked shouts boomed from two blocks away. Inn guests seated on the porch of White's Tavern sprang to their feet and rushed toward the square to see what was happening. All three boys ran in the direction of the alarm without any hesitation. E. Z. noticed that Mr. Burton stayed behind.

A crowd had already reassembled at the Court House. A man stood on a stump to announce to the crowd that deputies had captured the prisoner and they were bringing him in. Not only would his trial continue, but he would face charges for escape.

In a few minutes, a deputized storeowner rode into town leading a horse draped with a body and covered with a blanket. The crowd's chatter went silent as all eyes fixed on the body. There was clear disappointment that there would be no confrontation with the prisoner.

Isaiah joked, "Remind me to tell you how I captured the prisoner right after I tracked down Mr. Burton."

A deputy led the horse to the front door of the Court House and uncovered the body. The sheriff stepped forward to identify the prisoner. He studied the body and then looked up in surprise. "That's not him!"

The crowd gasped with a collective, "Who is he?" No one had ever seen him.

Except E. Z. The body was wearing the same coat as the body he had seen draped across the horse the night before in Nashville.

CHAPTER SIX

The Map

This time, E. Z. could not keep his secrets to himself. He had to tell the sheriff what he had seen. E. Z. sent the other boys back to the inn and waited for most of the crowd to leave the Court House. Once E. Z. finally found the sheriff alone, he mustered his courage and blurted out, "Sir, I know whose body is on the horse."

The sheriff seemed annoyed that E. Z. was distracting him from his investigation. "And whose body is it?"

"I don't know.... I mean. I have seen it before," E. Z. stammered.

"Son, you just told me that you know and now you are saying that you don't know. Can't you see that I am busy?" The sheriff looked at E. Z. closer. "I don't recognize you. Who is your father?"

"I'm not from around here. My father is dead," E. Z. said.

"Are you saying that was your father's body on the horse?" the sheriff said.

"No, Sir. My father died when I was young. We are passing through on the Natchez Trace. I saw that body on a horse Saturday night in Nashville."

"In Nashville?" The sheriff laughed, "Son, you can't believe all those stories people tell. Dead men don't ride horses from one town to the next—even on the Natchez Trace."

E. Z. grew frustrated, "I know dead people don't ride themselves. Someone put him on the horse and brought him down the Natchez Trace to Franklin."

"Now, who would go to all the trouble of putting a dead man on a horse just to give him one last pleasure ride to Franklin?" the sheriff asked.

"A bandit," E. Z. answered.

"A bandit, you say. Did you see a bandit kill that man?" the sheriff asked with a visible growing tension.

"No, Sir. But I saw him put the body on the horse. Or at least a body wearing those clothes."

"You would find several travelers in this area wearing those types of clothes. What time of the day did you see this?" the sheriff asked.

"It was in the night... or in the morning...about three in the morning. I was sleeping on the porch at the Nashville Inn, and.."

The sheriff interrupted E. Z., "It was dark. Yes, son, you were sleeping, and you dreamed it. And if you keep aggravating me with this nonsense, I'll give you the whipping that your father would give you if he was around. You may think you are just having some fun, but this is serious business. Now, are you traveling with your mother?"

E. Z. looked down, defeated. "Yess'r. She's at White's Tavern."

"You go there now! Do not pass this story along to anybody else along the way! And do not trouble me again!"

"But..." E. Z. continued.

"Do you hear me?" the sheriff shouted.

"Yess'r." E. Z. lowered his head and wandered back to the inn, deep in thought.

David and Isaiah ran out to meet him. Each talked over the other, "What did he say? Did he tell you who the man was? Did he give you any details?"

"No," E. Z. admitted. "He didn't believe me. He thought I was pulling a prank on him."

"Maybe you should tell your mother," Isaiah suggested.

"I can't. I told you. It would put her in danger," E. Z. said. "We will have to get more information ourselves before anyone will believe us. Are you with me?"

Both boys gave a half-nod.

"Good. We'll be leaving tomorrow. That gives us barely a few hours."

"To do what?" David asked.

"To look at that body," E. Z. replied.

"Are you telling me we are going out in the dark, by ourselves, and look for a dead body?" David asked a second time in disbelief, "In the dark?" Normally, he would have kept the covers pulled over his head until daylight at the mere thought of anything like a dead body being anywhere around.

"We have to know who it is if anyone is going to believe us," E. Z. answered.

Isaiah seemed to side with David. "If you believe some of the stories people tell about the Natchez Trace, we could just stay at the inn and that body would come looking for us."

"You can't believe *those* stories. The real ones are bad enough," E. Z. said.

Isaiah was not convinced. E. Z. was serious, and for once, Isaiah was too. "What do we have that will protect us out there in the dark? We don't know who or what we'll see."

"We have safety in numbers. Remember?" E. Z. reminded him.

David disagreed, "You and I may add up to the one man of our family, but we are all still no match for whatever might be out there in the dark."

"We will just have to be sure that they don't know we are there," E. Z. answered to put an end to any debate.

It was settled. The boys were going hunting for a dead body.

About midnight, the last inn guests finally finished their storytelling and went to sleep. At E. Z.'s signal, the boys rose and sneaked off the porch and down the street toward the rock bridge that led to the Natchez Trace. They had considered taking a lamp for light, but a full moon gave light bright enough to cast shadows of trees on the ground. The church and cemetery were not far down the road.

The innkeeper had said that town parson Reverend Blackburn had taken the body to the church. The body would rest there until a coffin could be built and until a proper burial could take place.

The boys walked past the cemetery that held the bodies of some of the Franklin town founders. They noticed a mound of dirt where someone had started digging a grave. E. Z. assumed that the grave was for the body brought in on the horse.

When David spotted the open grave, he moved to the opposite side of the road. He said he could imagine the body sitting up and reaching out to pull him down into the grave.

At the edge of the cemetery, the church building looked lonely in the moonlight. No lamps could be seen burning inside. An owl was the only living creature keeping watch in sight. It hooted at the boys and flew out of a tree by the church as they passed by. David jumped in fright. The owl seemed to take pleasure in scaring him. It lit again in the tree.

If the dead man had a family or friends nearby, they would have been sitting up with the body to safeguard it until time for burial. But no one knew who he was. E. Z. reasoned that bad men have no one to care for them when they die, because they did not care who they hurt while they lived.

E. Z. tugged at the church door, its hinges creaking with every inch as it opened.

"Loud enough to wake the dead," Isaiah joked.

As the boys walked through the door, David stayed close enough to E. Z. that he could have been his shadow in the moonlight. Isaiah put his hand on the door to shut it, until E. Z. whispered, "Don't. We may have to run out quick."

The boys looked down the aisle toward the front of the building. There it lay. The body.

It was stretched out on a board supported by two sawhorses. The arms were folded as if the dead man were sleeping. Moonlight streamed through the glass pane windows and reflected off white powder on the body's face making it glow in the dark.

Pieces of round metal, painted gold to look like coins, had been placed on the body's eyes to keep them closed. A ribbon was tied around the head to keep the mouth closed. The unworldly appearance would haunt David's dreams for weeks.

E. Z. noticed that the man was dressed to be buried in the same bright-colored outer coat that the bandit wore in Nashville. The body's coat had been covered with a blanket when they rode it into town.

The boys crept forward, making sure before taking each step that the body did not move. Sounds of the clunky thuds of their boots on the wooden floor were magnified off the wooden walls and ceiling. E. Z. held out his arm to slow the others to keep them from waking the body.

He stopped when he saw it. In the moonlight, the large scar across the face stood out. And the left ear was missing—It was the bandit they had seen at the Nashville Inn! He was dead!

Isaiah and David stood stunned. E. Z. looked around the room to see if the bandit's rat friends were protecting the body. "Keep a lookout for rats," he warned. Then, he walked up to the body and began feeling the coat.

"What are you doing?" Isaiah asked with disbelief.

"Your mother told my mother that on the Natchez Trace, people sew money into their clothes to hide it. Maybe he did the same thing," E. Z. said. He thought about the thin, gold object the bandit had showed him from outside the window at the inn in Nashville. He wanted to know what it was.

"Don't you think the sheriff already searched the body?" Isaiah asked.

"I interrupted him. He may not have gone back to finish," E. Z. answered.

"Go ahead. I'm right behind you," Isaiah said.

E. Z. paused. "Wait, I found something. He seems to be holding on to it." E. Z. had to move the man's hand to reach inside a slit in the coat, and he pulled out a folded piece of parchment.

E. Z. unfolded the parchment and walked over to the window to use the moonlight to reveal what was on it. "It's a map! There's an "X" on it."

The outside wooden step creaked. E. Z. turned to see the figure of a man standing at the open door of the church house. When the figure saw that E. Z. had spotted him, he ran. E. Z. rushed toward the door, but the figure was gone. The owl had returned. It must have seen the man, but it did not fly away.

"Did someone follow us? Has he been here all along?" The question echoed in the near-empty building.

"Maybe the map is one of those things that has a curse to punish whoever touches it. I have heard about those things. Put it back!" David said.

E. Z. agreed that he had no right to take the map. But it might tell them who the man was and what dangers they faced. He also considered that the map might lead to treasure.

E. Z. handed the map to David. "Do you think you can draw a copy of this map?"

David pushed it back. "I don't want to touch it. If you'll hold it, I can try."

E. Z. took David's drawing tablet and charcoal out of the hunting bag and handed them to David. David insisted that E. Z. position the map on the window to catch the light. As David scratched his charcoal against the page to copy the map, E. Z. stared outside the window to keep watch. Isaiah kept his eyes on the body to see if it moved.

When David finished, E. Z. folded up the copy and put it in the hunting bag. E. Z. then returned the map to the body. As he searched again for the slit in the coat, E. Z.'s hand brushed against the body's clammy hand.

"He still has his 'claws,'" E. Z. said, referring to the long fingernails.

As E. Z. struggled to push the map into the slit, the body's arm jerked. Its claws twitched across E. Z.'s hand, cutting three deep scratches. E. Z. looked to see if the face had changed expression or if the eyes had opened. Except for the arm, the body had not moved.

It took E. Z. a couple seconds to catch his breath. David and Isaiah stood frozen. They were too scared to say anything. E. Z. kept his wits and said, "It's just a natural reflex. I have heard about that happening."

E. Z. rubbed the scratches that were turning bright red and then continued searching the man's coat. The coat revealed no other secrets about who the bandit was. And it did not contain the thin, gold object the man had held up to the window outside the Nashville inn.

E. Z. stood back, looked at the body, and bragged, "This is the last time you will threaten me, Sir." Without thinking, E. Z. emphasized his point by adding, "Bandit" and kicking one of the sawhorses holding the board. The kick was harder than E. Z. intended, and the jolt jarred the body.

The bandit's foot moved first, starting spasms that ran up his leg and throughout the whole body. His arms and legs began flailing wildly. As the sound of the board bouncing on the sawhorses grew louder and reached a crescendo, the body sat up.

The metal pieces fell off the body's eyes and clanked as they rolled across the wooden floor. The eyelids fluttered open. Ribbon holding the jaw loosened. The mouth opened and escaping air made a loud groan, "Ooooowwww!"

E. Z. did not wait for David to scream in response before he put his hand across David's mouth. "It's just a reflex," E. Z. said calmly as he took two steps backward, and then shouted, "but RUN!!"

Isaiah and David needed no encouragement. The boys' feet never touched the wooden steps as they flew out of the church. David almost hit the owl that joined them in taking flight in fright.

With Isaiah in the lead, the boys tore back toward the inn. Dogs began barking in the distance behind them.

"Somebody is following us!" E. Z. said.

"*Some*body? I know *whose* body is following us!" Isaiah said.

"The bandit is coming after us for the map!" David said. David was normally slowest in races, but he began running faster, taking the lead.

Once E. Z. was safely beyond the reach of the body, his thoughts turned to the map. He could barely wait to examine it.

David quietly opened the back door of White's Tavern. The innkeeper had left a grease lamp burning in the common room on a table next to a clay jug of cold water, in case any guests became thirsty during the night. The boys were drawn like moths to the light to study the map.

E. Z. unfolded David's drawing and held it up to the flame. The main image was four snakes. The head of one snake was at the top and right of the page and its tail ran across the page to the bottom on the left side. The second went from left to right on the page. Its head was on the left, and the lower part of its body ran up and down. The third snake became part of the second and its tail made it appear as it the snake on the left were moving. A fourth smaller snake was crawling out of its mouth. Just below, there was an inverted "U" with an "X" inside. The bottom part of the map was missing.

"What language is that?" Isaiah asked.

"I couldn't tell what it was supposed to be. Two snakes crossways. Maybe the snakes stand for bandits and it says that two bandits got crossways with each other and buried something where the 'X' is," David said.

"Are you sure you copied it right? Your hands were shaking pretty bad," E. Z. joked.

"So were Isaiah's, and he wasn't even trying to draw," David said.

"Maybe it's Indian writing, like they used to draw on caves," Isaiah said.

E. Z. disagreed, "No. I think this is a map to something the bandit wanted to find. But how do we start trying to figure it out?"

The back door began rattling and its latch moved up and down. David said, "The bandit's body is trying to get in! See! I told you! It followed us!"

The rattling stopped. The door jerked open. Instead of the body, Mr. Burton walked in. "I thought I heard you boys in here. What are you doing up?" He stepped over to the water jug and took a cup. "Did you hear those dogs barking? They woke me up, and I came inside to get some cold water. It hasn't cooled down all night." The boys noticed that Mr. Burton was sweating again.

"We were just talking," David said.

"I thought I saw you reading something. What are you looking at?" Mr. Burton asked.

"Something I drew," David said.

"I'd like to see your drawing. What did you do with it?" Mr. Burton asked.

"We've formed a club. It would break the rules to show someone who's not a member," E. Z. said.

"Perhaps I can join. I have belonged to clubs. I can keep all the club secrets," Mr. Burton said.

"I'm sorry, Mr. Burton. You're too old for this club," E. Z. said. "And you have to be invited."

Mr. Burton finished his water and looked to David and Isaiah for encouragement. When they did not counter E. Z.'s answer, Mr. Burton gave up and turned to walk to the porch. E. Z. added, "But I was wondering something. Do you always sleep with your boots on?"

David and Isaiah looked down at Mr. Burton's boots.

Mr. Burton smiled, "Well, very often, I do. I do not trust the people who sleep at these inns enough to leave my boots unattended while I sleep. It will be daylight soon. You boys had better get some sleep of your own. Now, keep that drawing safe. We will be heading out down the Natchez Trace after sunrise." Mr. Burton walked out and shut the door.

Isaiah asked, "Did you see the mud on his boots?"

E. Z. said," Yes. It was fresh."

"Maybe he saw who was following us," David offered.

E. Z. replied, "Maybe he did, and maybe he didn't." E. Z. suddenly realized that he was quoting what the bandit had said at the inn. He assured himself that the bandit was not speaking in his head.

E. Z. looked down at the copy of the map in his hands and thought about the curse David kept mentioning. Then, he looked at the red scratches on his hand. He worried they would never heal. Had the bandit "branded" him for taking a copy of the map?

CHAPTER SEVEN

The Test

_____

At daybreak, the boys joined their party for breakfast in the common room. E. Z. thought of a plan. "I think we should store David's drawing tablet in Ma's trunks for safekeeping." He made the announcement loud enough to be overheard by any of the other guests who would be interested.

Isaiah caught on to what E. Z. had in mind, but his attempt to help only made the plan less credible. "Why don't you store the drawing tablet in your mother's trunk?"

E. Z. replied with some frustration, "That's what I will do."

E. Z. walked into the small baggage room at the rear of the inn, leaving the door slightly ajar where he could be seen. The room was stacked high with guests' trunks and bags. E. Z. found one of his mother's trunks and opened it. As E. Z. leaned over the trunk with his back to the door, he placed the map David had drawn of the Cumberland River in the hunting bag. He slipped the copy of the bandit's map out of the hunting bag and put it in his boot. Then, he turned toward the door and made a show of putting the drawing tablet into the trunk.

E. Z. returned to the table in the common room. "All done. It should be safe in there."

The boys ran outside and jumped onto the wagon to ride with Mr. Johnson and Major to a Franklin store to load flour and bacon for the next leg of their trip. Sarah joined the Stewarts to walk the two blocks to meet them at the store to see what other goods they should add.

The store was small but packed with an assortment of goods needed on the frontier—nails, glass, buttons, and writing paper, as well as food. E. Z. noticed Sarah running her hand over bolts of expensive cloth. She may have imagined making fine dresses. Instead, Sarah bought straw hats for the boys to wear. She said that the sun would pickle them within a day riding out in the open. Both boys chose hats that looked closest to the one that Mr. Johnson wore.

Captain Stark entered, whistling a tune from the Revolution. He said that finally heading south and closer to their future homes had given him new energy. The captain seemed to be the only one in their group with money to spare. Before leaving home, he said, he had sold land in the Ohio River Valley that the government had given him for his service in the war.

The captain offered to take charge of final preparations for the journey he often called "marching into battle." The captain said that he wanted to make sure that they had all the necessities to keep everyone comfortable. His ideas were different than the women's. The soldier bought coffee, a block of tea, and a pack of cards. He was shocked at the price of sugar and decided that they could make do with half of what he had planned. He added a small box with a lock to safeguard it.

Captain Stark noticed Hannah eying candy jars on the counter. She said Mary had warned her not to ask for luxuries. They would have only enough money for what they needed. The captain wanted to share his mood of celebration, telling the storeowner to bag up enough candy sticks for all the children to have a few pieces.

The captain handed the bag to E. Z. "Ezekiel, I'm making you quartermaster over these supplies. Dispense them slowly so that they last. I doubt there will be anyplace else to buy more for a long time."

E. Z. smiled from the confidence that the captain had placed in him. He assured himself that he would guard the candy with his life. He deposited the bag of candy in the hunting bag on top of David's map of the Cumberland River.

"Where are you headed?" the storeowner asked.

Captain Stark said, "The Mississippi Territory. We hear there is good farmland selling cheap."

"Watch out for scoundrels selling land they don't own. A lot of people like you are heading southwest with money, and money attracts people who want to take it," the store owner said.

"Does that include bandits?" E. Z. asked.

"Especially bandits," the store owner answered as he wrapped up the last of the purchases in paper and tied each package with a string. "Bandits come in all forms. Some have been living out of society so long that you might mistake them for some of the animals in the woods. Others are dressed like the finest Philadelphia lawyers. Both want your money. And both will do whatever it takes to get it."

Sarah frowned. "Who enforces the law on the Natchez Trace?"

The storekeeper laughed at the idea. "Federal rangers ride it. There aren't many though. You'll see garrisons near Bentontown, Gordon's Ferry, Grindstone Ford, and all the way west in Natchez. In between those forts, it will mainly be up to you."

"But there are a lot of people traveling the road, aren't there?" Sarah asked.

"At times. Though you will go through long stretches without seeing anyone. Bandits know the areas where travelers normally slow down or camp, and they wait there until they catch travelers alone," he said.

Sarah put her hand to her mouth. "Oh my. We heard in Nashville that it was dangerous, but I don't think we expected that we would be alone on the road."

The storekeeper said, "A lot of people don't expect the dangers on the Natchez Trace, and they don't make it."

He pointed over to Captain Stark. "At least you have a soldier with you. Your driver can take care of himself. Do you have other men going with you?"

"Mary's husband John and Mr. Burton, Joshua Burton," Sarah said.

"Joshua Burton, Joshua Burton," the storeowner said as he scratched his head in thought. "Probably a common name… Anyway, it's good that you have some protection." Looking at E. Z., he added, "And your boy there should be able to help."

"He is tall for his age. I am afraid his father did not live long enough to teach him those kinds of things," Sarah said.

E. Z. glanced up, embarrassed.

The storeowner gave E. Z. a determined look. "He will have to learn fast where you are headed.

The boys followed the storeowner outside to help load the items the women had purchased.

The merchant thanked the party and apologized. "I'm sorry that my helper hasn't come in yet today. Everybody is a little distracted by that body brought into town last night."

E. Z. asked, "Have they found out who it was?"

The storeowner said, "No. But the bigger question is what happened to it. It has disappeared."

The boys stopped loading. "Disappeared?" David asked.

"Reverend Blackburn had the body taken to the church building until a burial. When they finished the coffin and took it down there today, the body was gone," he added.

"I told you it was following us. It was coming for the map!" David whispered to E. Z.

Captain Stark was puzzled. "Maybe he had family that came and claimed it to bury it."

"They didn't report it to anybody if they did. It's a mystery. Some folks are suggesting that he wasn't dead after all and got up and walked off. That has been known to happen. People are uneasy that he still could be around."

"I knew it!" David said out loud as everyone turned to look at him, and then just as quickly ignored the outburst.

Sarah said, "Maybe it is a good thing we are leaving today."

E. Z. whispered to David and Isaiah, "That depends on where he went."

The store owner waived goodbye to the travelers. "Don't forget. Bandits come in all forms. Your driver will tell you." Mr. Johnson nodded and grunted in agreement.

Mr. Johnson drove the wagon back to White's Tavern. When the boys went to the rear room to retrieve their parents' belongings, they saw the Perkins' family belongings strewn on the floor. Both of Sarah's trunks were open. A few pages from David's drawing tablet were ripped into shreds. And in the center of it all sat Mr. Burton.

Mr. Burton looked up, startled to see the group. "Just look at this mess. Those dogs we heard barking last night must have chased a rabbit or something into here and made a wreck of things to catch it."

David looked around the room and whispered to E. Z.," My drawing paper! Do you have the bandit's map in the hunting bag?"

E. Z. whispered, "It's in my boot."

Sarah began to cry. "This is everything we have."

Mary comforted her. "I'm sure it is all still here. It is just scattered. I don't see how dogs opened trunks. It looks more like someone was looking for something."

"Do you think the bandit came looking for the map?" Isaiah whispered.

"I think it may have been a bandit," E. Z. answered quietly, looking at Mr. Burton. He thought Mr. Burton had been clever to talk about dogs as suspects. The boys did not want their parents to know that they had sneaked away the night before.

Mr. Burton overheard E. Z. and said, "It was a good thing I came in when I did, then. I must have scared him off."

"We should call for the sheriff," Sarah said.

"No need if everything is here," Mr. Burton said. He looked at E. Z. and David. "Are you missing anything, boys?"

E. Z. did not want another threat of a whipping by the sheriff. "No. I'm sure it's still here. Don't cry, Ma. We'll help you gather everything."

Mr. Burton worked quicker than anyone else to help Sarah repack. After the travelers' belongings had been loaded into the wagon and everyone had boarded,

Mr. Johnson began his song to the oxen to drive the wagon from Franklin. Mr. Burton followed on Esther.

E. Z. wondered whether they were leaving the body behind. Occasionally, he glanced back, expecting to see it following them on the road.

But what he feared most was waiting ahead for them down the Natchez Trace.

CHAPTER EIGHT

Bentontown

After the wagon crossed the rock bridge leading to the Natchez Trace, the boys kept a lookout for the escaped prisoner ahead on the road. And, of course, for Jack.

For the next two hours, the wagon passed scattered farms. Then, a small settlement came into view.

Mr. Johnson said, "This here is Hillsboro, but some folks call it 'Bentontown.' One woman, Nancy Benton, owns the whole town. We'll stop here fer water and fer an early dinner. Then we'll git to the part of the Natchez Trace you boys have been worryin' me about."

Mr. Johnson pulled the wagon to a stop by the Benton spring. A few travelers could be heard talking and laughing as they watered their horses at a stream nearby called "Murphy's Fork."

Sarah and Mary looked for a good place to spread blankets for their meal. After finding a cool, shady area near the creek, they told the children to run around until their dinner was ready. They had been cramped in the wagon all morning.

At first, the children did not see much that took their interest. Bentontown appeared to be mainly a schoolhouse, a warehouse, and a mill. The Benton house, situated on a small hill by the road, had two main rooms on the first floor that were separated by a wide breezeway porch. What took the children's attention was that the main part of the house was resting on a cellar that rose up out of the ground.

Isaiah spotted windows with bars across them at ground level. "It's a jail," he said. The children saw several travelers with guns coming out of the cellar that was the same level as the road.

"The bandits are escaping! If only the sheriff had deputized me last night, I could stop them," he joked.

"Go ahead. I am friends with the sheriff now," E. Z. said as both boys laughed.

One man untied his horse and rode up to the children. He slowed the pace and stared at E. Z.'s bag as he passed him, then stopped. When the man raised his head, E. Z. could see under the long, floppy brim of the man's hat that a black patch covered his left eye. "Where'd you get that bag, boy?" the man growled.

"A boatman gave it to me," E. Z. said.

"Boatman? On the Cumberland?" the man asked.

"Yes, Sir."

"Why did he give it to *you*?" the man asked.

"I don't know. He said I would need it."

"Leave that boy alone—for now," the man's riding partner yelled out as he waited for him.

"I suppose we'll both find out soon enough," the man said as he kicked the sides of his horse and rode away.

"I hope that everybody we meet is not as rude as that man," Hanna said.

"Why was he interested in the bag?" David asked.

"Maybe he knew the last man who carried it," E. Z. said.

"Maybe he recognized the blood," Isaiah joked.

The strange man and bars on the windows only made the boys more curious about what was inside the cellar.

As they got close to the house, the children smelled food cooking. The aromas reminded them of the Nashville Inn when dinner was being cooked at the fireplace.

The boys leaned close to the windows trying to peer into the darker area inside. A loud, commanding voice startled them, "Do strangers peep in your windows where you come from?" They turned to see a stout woman with her hands on her hips a few steps behind them.

Hannah was first to speak. "We were just seeing what was cooking. It smelled so good from across the road, and we are so hungry."

The woman looked over to the spring where the children's mothers were spreading out a simple dinner on a blanket on the grass. It was clear that there was not enough to give the children a full meal.

The woman's stern expression changed to a smile. "I did not mean to scare you. I just came out to ask you to be my guests. We have not entertained as many travelers as we expected today. We have plenty."

David whispered to E. Z., "I don't want to go down there. She looks like a witch. She will keep us as her prisoners in that jail."

Hannah overheard. She laughed and whispered, "Doesn't a witch have better things to do than spend her time feeding strangers all day?"

"Didn't your mother ever read you the story about the witch baking children in her ovens?" David asked. "The witch first invited them into her house to eat."

E. Z. ignored David's worries and told the woman, "We'll have to ask our mothers first."

"Of course," the woman said. "My invitation was for you all. Run ask your mothers."

David pleaded with E. Z., "It's a trap. The food is just bait to get us inside those bars." E. Z. ignored him.

A few minutes later, Hannah returned. "My Ma says that we can't afford to eat here. We have to save our money."

David looked relieved.

The woman persisted, "I understand. Please tell your mother that I am not charging anything. You will save me from throwing out perfectly good food to the dogs. I have prepared too much."

After Hannah ran back and forth, the woman finally sent E. Z. to tell their mothers that she never took a "no" for an answer. She was setting a meal for them, and she expected them to eat with her.

Sarah and Mary agreed to pack up their meal for another time and accept the offer. Mary assured Sarah that the offer was not charity, but hospitality. Besides, they did not know when the children might have another good meal cooked at a hearth.

Mr. Johnson stayed behind to feed and water the oxen. He offered to take care of the horse also, but Mr. Burton insisted that he would remain behind to take care of Esther and stretch his legs along the creek.

Mr. Burton seemed perturbed that Mrs. Benton had invited the party inside for a meal. He had made it clear that he had no intention of going inside. E. Z. wondered what disagreement Mr. Burton had with the Bentons.

The woman held out her hand as the party approached and introduced herself, "I am "Nancy Benton." Please be my guests. You are coming from the East, and it would do me good to get some news from there."

As they entered the cellar door into the dark underground room, David walked close to his brother. The room was cool underground, a good place to eat dinner on a hot day. The floor was lined with brick. The cellar had a damp, earthy smell, but one mixed with the savory scents of food cooked over the hearth.

Mrs. Benton's servants brought in several dishes of pork, summer vegetables, and cornbread and lined them in the center of the long tables. Mrs. Benton seated herself at one end. She said that her son would be joining her. He could sit at the other end. The children had their own table.

As the traveling party ate, Mrs. Benton told her guests the story of her husband's death in North Carolina. She had raised small children alone without him. Rather than remaining in an area that she knew as home, she had set out with her children to Tennessee and bought this large farm. Because the land had been at the virtual border with the Indian nations, it was cheap. Land values would rise once new settlers considered the area safe. It would be a good investment for her children's future.

E. Z. noticed that Sarah ate little. She seemed mesmerized by Mrs. Benton's advice. His mother would be in the same position as Mrs. Benton—taking her sons to the edge of the frontier. E. Z. could see a new confidence in his mother's eyes as she soaked up assurance from Ms. Benton.

Sarah said, "We were surprised to learn that the Natchez Trace is so dangerous. The children have asked our wagon driver, Mr. Johnson, hundreds of questions about bandits and Indians."

"You are wise to be concerned," Mrs. Benton said. "The dangers are real. You should expect that some thief in Nashville studied your party to decide whether he would follow you down the Natchez Trace. But you don't seem to be carrying anything that would make it worth his time.

"I should say not. He would be disappointed how little we are carrying," Sarah replied. She did not know about the knife and the map.

Mrs. Benton continued, "You can't give in to every scoundrel who tries to take advantage of you. You have to be smarter and tougher than they are." Her stern tone suggested that she was speaking from experience.

She continued, "Out here, everybody will test you to see how strong you are. You just make it known from the start that you will NOT BACK DOWN!" Even Captain Stark instinctively jumped in surprise as Mrs. Benton hit the table to emphasize her point.

Mrs. Benton looked over to the children and joked, "I don't have to paint *my* face like an Indian warrior to frighten people. This face seems to be scary enough." She laughed.

Isaiah whispered to E. Z., "We should take Mrs. Benton along to fight off the bandits and Indian warriors."

E. Z. laughed and whispered, "She and Mr. Johnson would make a powerful army. But they are both so ornery that they would do more damage to each other than a bandit. They would be better off alone."

E. Z. wondered whether his mother would become the hardened old woman that he saw in Mrs. Benton after Sarah had spent a lifetime on the frontier.

Mrs. Benton's son, Thomas Hart Benton, entered and sat at the large table within a short distance from the children. His clothes were almost as fancy as Mr. Burton's. E. Z. recognized him as one of the judges he had seen at the trial.

Mrs. Benton encouraged the children, "Thomas can tell you what you need to know about the Natchez Trace. He worked as a clerk at the storehouse at Gordon's Ferry before he read the law and became judge."

The judge looked up from his plate, annoyed that he was expected to take time from his meal to talk with children. He made it clear that he spoke to them only to please his mother. "Mother has given you sound advice, and I am wise enough never to contradict my mother."

Speaking to E. Z. as the tallest child, he said, "That is my advice. Follow it and you'll at least be safe from the one who can harm you most." The judge snatched a piece of bread and immediately rose and walked out to keep from being bothered further.

Mrs. Benton seemed a little embarrassed at her son's response. She said, "Once you have made your farms safe from the dangers, you might consider spending more time teaching good manners than I did."

E. Z. asked, "Mrs. Benton, may I ask you a question?"

"Of course."

"When we arrived here, we met a man who was wearing a patch over his eye. He was just leaving. Do you know who he was?"

Mrs. Benton shook her head. "I am afraid not. I don't know most of the travelers who pass through here. But they know about me!" she laughed. "I make sure that other stand owners along the Natchez Trace spread the word that I don't put up with any foolishness here. It works. They are careful to be on their best behavior when they walk through *my* door."

After everyone had finished eating, Mrs. Benton gave the mothers bundles of food left over from the meal. She told her servants to add extra packages of salted bacon from her smokehouse.

Sarah hesitated a few minutes to survey the Benton farm before she boarded the wagon. E. Z. could see that his mother was imagining running her own farm south in the Mississippi Territory.

David noticed it too, and he pulled out his tablet and drew a picture of the barn. The small door for the hay loft that jutted out from the top reminded him of a castle he had read about in a book about British wars. "We could hold off a whole party of invaders from that position," he told E. Z. as he showed him the drawing.

It was a good suggestion. E. Z. thought they might have to fight off lots of invaders at their new home along the Natchez Trace.

CHAPTER NINE

The Gate to the Wilderness

Not long after the wagon left the Benton farm, the party came to a large stone bridge over a stream. A worker walked out of a little shed to collect money. The man who had built the bridge made everyone pay a toll to cross it.

"How much today?" Mr. Johnson asked.

"Two bits," the operator said.

Mr. Johnson grumbled to the boys as his large hands fumbled to open a cloth money bag, "See, bandits do come in all forms. That's highway robbery!"

The heavy timbers of the toll bridge rumbled like thunder as the iron rims of the wagon wheels ran across it. When the rumbling stopped, Mr. Johnson halted the wagon. "Now right here's whar we'll run into The Wilderness."

The boys lifted their hats to see a steep road running up the side of a bluff. At the top, trees grew thick. Their limbs made an arch over the road, creating a door to The Wilderness. It was a fitting entrance to the road boatmen described as "mysterious."

Mr. Johnson continued, "Folks, facts of the matter is that we have to go up thar, about 200 feet up. I won't take any chances of the wagon rollin' back down the hill and killin' anybody. Everybody off! Let me git to the top first and then, follow me up the hill on foot."

Major jumped off the wagon with the boys.

"Major! Yo're on duty. Git back up here!" Mr. Johnson shouted. The dog ran and jumped back on. When the others had dismounted the wagon, Mr. Johnson gave the command and began singing his song to the oxen.

The oxen grunted and snorted as they strained to pull the wagon loaded with the party's belongings up the hill. Mr. Johnson slowed at times to give the oxen extra encouragement. As he promised, Mr. Johnson stopped the wagon at the top to wait for everyone to board it again. He shouted down the hill with a boom that carried across the valley, "Alright, folks. The oxes did it. People next."

Mr. Burton had more trouble persuading Esther to ride up the hill. E. Z. knew that if Sarah and the boys had not been watching him, Mr. Burton might have taken out his rawhide whip to threaten her. Instead, he followed Mr. Johnson's example and tried encouraging the horse.

Mr. Burton used soft, exaggerated encouragement, "Come along darling," as he gently kicked her sides. "There you go, you beautiful vision." Hannah giggled and began calling Mr. Burton's encouragement "sweet talk."

Hannah asked Sarah playfully, "Do you suppose Mr. Burton talks to *all* his 'girls' that way?"

Sarah blushed.

The boys ran a foot race to the top to prove who could arrive first. After Sarah stopped a few times panting and fanning her face with a decorated fan, E. Z. returned to encourage his mother by walking with her. Sometimes, E. Z. put his hand on Sarah's back to give her a pat, but also to use his strength to help push her forward.

Sarah laughed, "Goodness. I don't know why I am out of breath. I must have eaten more than I thought at Mrs. Benton's. Her cooking was too delicious."

All the grownups were panting by the time they reached the top of the ridge. They took a moment to rest. Mr. Burton helped Sarah to a stump where she could sit for a few minutes before boarding the wagon.

"Folks, look back yonder," Mr. Johnson said, pointing to Bentontown behind them. "That's the last time you'll see a town 'til we cross the Tennessee River to Colbert's. Now, this here is the best chance you'll have to turn back. If you change yore mind down the trail, yo're on yore own. Speak now or hold yore peace."

Mr. Burton wiped his forehead, pulled at his collar, and said with anger, "You could have told them that before they had all the trouble of walking up this hill. The best place to turn back was down there."

Mr. Johnson did not back down. "You'd be surprised at the people who hire me for this trip who can't git up that hill. If they can't make it this fer, they won't make it very fer on the Natchez Trace, and I don't take 'em. That'd be murder. Folks, this trip ain't easy, but I suspect all y'all know that by now."

Mr. Burton continued to argue, "Why do you let your passengers get this far before you tell them they can't make the trip? Could you not warn them back at Nashville?"

"Yep," Mr. Johnson said. "But 'til they try to make it up that hill, they don't believe me." Then with a grin he added, "Besides, once they git this fer, thar's no refunds."

Mr. Johnson looked to the whole party. "Alright folks, the oxes is rested and if you are too, let's make some distance before dark sets in."

All the adults agreed that too much had been invested to turn back. After mounting the wagon, they chanced their futures rolling south through the dark forest and thick brush.

It was probably E. Z.'s imagination but knowing that he was now in The Wilderness made everything look and sound strange. The calls of ravens or crows from hollows below them serenaded them with haunting music. Thick foliage often blocked their views. When E. Z. was able to look up through the tree canopy to see the sky, he spotted vultures that seemed to be following them in anticipation of a meal.

Occasionally, the boys were able to look down into the valleys and see for a great distance. E. Z. figured out that the long ridge where the road ran on top was shaped just like a man's spine, a backbone. Now, the "Backbone" part of the name "The Devil's Backbone" that the wild-eyed boatman had warned him about made sense.

Mr. Johnson pointed to a fort. "Look down yonder. That's one of them outposts soldiers built to protect Nashville. That garrison still has a few soldiers. It's seen its share of attacks by Creek Indians."

David stopped drawing. "Are Creek Indians still around?"

"Creek and Shawnee parties come through here. They've not attacked in some time. If we see any on the road, be careful to do nothin' that would make 'em think you wanna attack. That goes fer all the Indians."

"But you're a good shot, aren't you Mr. Johnson?" Isaiah asked.

"Not good enough to take on a whole party of Indians. Thar's a lot more of 'em than us. Keep that in mind."

"How many Indians have you seen?" David asked.

"Oh, I'd say hundreds," Mr. Johnson said.

"How many eyes do they have?" David prodded.

"Eyes?" Mr. Johnson asked.

"I've heard that Indians have eyes in the back of their head. They can see everywhere," David said.

"Indians ain't no different than you 'n me. Two eyes, two ears, two legs, and so on. They use theirs better than we do in the woods. It just *seems* that they've got more than their share."

"How do they do that?" Isaiah asked.

"Oh, from the time they are 'bout yore age, boys are trained to be warriors. They study the woods so that they can blend into 'em and not be seen. Then they study the animals in the woods. And they learn to be just like 'em. They watch what the animals eat, how they hunt their prey, how they build their nests or beds to sleep. Them Indian warriors can move through the woods so quiet that no one suspects they're thar. Facts of the matter, they could have us surrounded right now, and we wouldn't know."

At that, David began looking for Indians behind every tree. He imagined that Indians had disguised themselves as trees, and E. Z. had to assure him that a tree was just a tree.

Mr. Johnson tried to calm him. "But the Indians are at peace now. Leastways, as fer as I know. Usually, they don't attack unless their red king, or war king, has decided they have grounds to go to war. Yo're more likely to be attacked by a bandit. The problem is that bandits sometimes disguise themselves as Indians."

"That doesn't seem fair," Isaiah said.

Mr. Johnson agreed. "It's an easy way for bandits to put the blame on somebody else. Some folks don't like Indians. A lot more are afraid of 'em. The guilty men blame Indians even for things the Indians don't do, and other folks are quick to believe the stories. Then the guilty men are free to keep robbin'."

"But are there bad Indians too?" E. Z. asked.

Mr. Johnson thought a moment and said, "Thar's good and bad in every nation. Men are men ever'whar. Our skin won't change what's in our hearts. I've seen the best and worst in all kinds of men."

"What about women?" E. Z. asked.

"Women? Hmm. Now, that's a deeper well. I'm no expert thar," Mr. Johnson said. "That'd be a question for your mother."

E. Z. whispered to Isaiah that his assessment of Mr. Johnson and Mrs. Benton ever teaming up had been correct.

After the travelers had been riding a few hours, the sun still was far from setting on the long summer day. But Mr. Johnson pulled the wagon over on the side of the road and came to a stop.

"We'll make camp right here. The oxes is gettin' hungry and tired. And that makes seven of us."

Mr. Johnson spoke to the whole group, "Now, folks, do as you please, but lots'a folks bury their money durin' the night. If bandits attack us, it'll be harder fer 'em to make off with your valuables if they have to hunt fer 'em."

Captain Stark pondered a few minutes and then he walked into the woods by himself. E. Z. watched to see whether Mr. Burton would follow him, but he showed no interest. Mr. Burton did not go into the woods to bury any money. Isaiah's father did go into the woods.

The women decided that they would keep their money in their dresses where they had sewn it. E. Z. thought it odd that Mr. Stewart went into the woods if Mrs. Stewart was carrying their money.

Isaiah distracted E. Z.'s study of his traveling companions. "Let's play a game of battle," he shouted from the edge of the woods. E. Z. and David smiled and ran toward him.

"What about me?" Hannah asked.

Isaiah said, "A girl can't be a soldier. You can be a defenseless settler. I'll be the army that is trying to attack you, and David can be the army that protects you. E. Z. is on my side."

"Why are you trying to attack me? I'm your sister," Hanna said.

"You're not my sister in the battle game."

Hannah shook her finger. "Alright. But I'm warning you. I know that frontier women fight back. You try to attack me, and I'll make you wish you had left the settlers alone!"

The game went on until time for supper. David built a small fort from logs in the woods, but he refused to allow a girl inside it. Hannah was forced to build her own house. David only came out of his fort when they were under attack.

Hannah made good on her threat. Each time Isaiah and E. Z. got close, she pelted them with green apples she found on one of the trees near her house. David helped her, but he seemed more concerned about protecting his fort than the settlers.

Mr. Johnson ended the battle when he summoned the boys to build a campfire. They disappointed him by admitting that none of them had any idea where to start.

Mr. Johnson shook his head, but he was patient. "Now, see those limbs on the ground? You'd probably reach fer 'em first, 'cause they would be easier to pick up, wouldn't you?"

The boys nodded.

"You gotta gather dead limbs hangin' from trees first. They are drier. Wood on the ground holds water from rains and that makes it harder to start your fire. Then, you gather pine needles and straw, 'tinder.' Real thin. They'll catch fire quick and that fire will start to burn the limbs. Then the limbs'll burn the heavy wood. If you try burnin' the limbs first, they'll never catch fire."

When the boys had gathered limbs and Hannah had found tinder, Mr. Johnson stacked the limbs in a pile and slid tinder underneath. He took a silver cloth he called a "flint cloth" out of his pocket. "Watch this," he said.

He struck two pieces of the cloth together and sparks flew from it. The sparks lit the tinder and in a few minutes, fire from the tinder was burning the limbs and then limbs started burning the heavier wood."

"Natchez Trace mystery," Isaiah joked.

Mr. Johnson took an iron tripod he called "crossbars" out of the wagon and set it up over the fire. He showed the women how to use it to hang their pots over the fire to cook.

The party gathered around the campfire to eat their supper and to talk about the day's events. After supper, Mr. Johnson said, "Thar's a good spring just down the hill. Boys, take some buckets and go down thar and fill 'em up with water to wash the dishes."

The boys hiked down the hill through thick brush, banging their wooden buckets against the trees on their way down. They scared three deer that ran in the opposite direction and stopped at the edge of the clearing. A young fawn stood still and stared at them.

As the boys positioned the buckets to catch water from the spring, E. Z. spotted two shiny metal objects sticking out of the dirt. "Look. Is that gold?" He reached down and dug two pieces of metal out with a stick. He let out a sigh when he saw that they were painted tin.

Isaiah laughed, "Your boatman was right. On the Natchez Trace, nothing is real." He flung the gold tin up with his stick in disappointment. "It's playing with us," he added, as if to suggest that the mysterious road was alive.

"They're real enough for me. I'll take them," David said, and he picked them up and put them in E. Z.'s hunting bag. When the other boys looked at him with disbelief, he said, "They may fool a robber and buy our way out of trouble."

The other boys nodded that David had a point.

Isaiah asked, "Do you think people bury their money in the woods to hide it from bandits and then leave it behind when bandits scare them away?"

E. Z. said, "I'm sure that happens. Maybe the bandits plan it that way."

"I hope nobody lost his life for that Natchez Trace gold. Look it over for blood," Isaiah joked, but David pulled them out to search for blood.

E. Z. stared at the gold pieces. "I've been thinking that those look like the pieces that were on the body's eyes back at the church. But how could they get here?"

Deer suddenly charged toward the boys as if they were being chased by a larger animal. Isaiah had to move to avoid being run over. He said, "I've never seen deer do that. Something must have scared them a lot more that we did for them to run toward us. What do you think it is? A bear?" E. Z. thought of the hairy creature he had seen, but he did not want to scare David any more than he was already.

"Maybe it's a party of Creek Indians, and we just can't see them," David suggested. His imagination grew, "Or maybe that body is following us." David looked down to the metal pieces. "Does he want these back?" He threw them on the ground and shouted, "I'm leaving them here where we found them."

The cedar trees were thick enough that the boys could not see whether someone was standing within reach. E. Z. looked toward the spot where the deer had been standing and strained his eyes. He could barely make out something glistening as it reflected the setting sun in the dusk. He remembered the way the silver band on Jack's hat had shined on the Public Square in Nashville.

That must be it. Jack was there! Maybe he was the one following them.

"Come on! Let's get back to camp as fast as we can! Don't look back!"

The boys scrambled up the hill. They couldn't wait to tell Mr. Johnson that they had seen someone in the woods.

The men and boys sat around the campfire and discussed plans to coordinate their defense. Mr. Johnson said, "The men'll need to take turns as camp watchman tonight. I'll go first so I can get some sleep near sunup."

"What do we do if we see someone?" E. Z. asked.

Mr. Johnson said, "If it's a small number, you let us handle it. If thar's more, everybody'll have to join in. Use whatever you can put your hands on to defend yourselves. That's how it's done." Mr. Johnson talked calmly about the chance of being attacked in camp as if it were as common as eating supper.

The man selected to be camp watchman would have the job of keeping the campfire burning to scare away the wild animals. E. Z. worried that the light would help bandits see everyone in camp.

The boys again had trouble sleeping. They listened for every sound in the dark of the woods, and all the animals that came out at night kept them guessing.

About midnight, a piercing cry shattered the silence. It sounded like a baby crying deep in the woods.

E. Z. sprang up and saw that Mr. Johnson was still serving as watchman. "What's a baby doing in the woods?"

Mr. Johnson answered, "That's no baby. It's a bobcat. You'd better get used to that sound or you'll be awake all night."

"A bobcat? Won't it try to attack us?" David asked.

Mr. Johnson answered, "It might. But it'll be afeared of the fire. We just need to be sure to keep a good fire burnin'." He swatted his neck. "The fire'll help keep these skeeters away, too."

Mr. Burton's turn was from two a.m. to sunrise. Even as Mr. Johnson slept, he kept his pistol by his side. It was clear that he was expecting trouble. E. Z. woke often to see whether Mr. Burton was still at his post. A couple times, E. Z. spotted him walking outside the camp, but Mr. Burton did not leave.

In the morning, as the women worked at the campfire boiling coffee, making biscuits, and frying Mrs. Benton's bacon, the boys walked back to the spring to fetch water to wash the dishes. E. Z. spotted fresh horse tracks. Someone had been close to camp. The painted metal pieces were gone.

The boys ran back up the hill to tell Mr. Johnson. Mr. Johnson and Captain Stark were coming out of the woods. The captain gloated, "It's an old trick I learned in the army. I didn't know whether anyone was watching me, but I couldn't take any chances."

Captain Stark told the boys that he had only pretended to bury his money in the woods. His trick had worked. Someone had dug up the spot he had selected only to be disappointed that it was empty.

Was it Jack with the silver band on his hat? Or was it someone in the traveling party?

E. Z. thought of the map. Maybe that is what they were waiting for. He made plans to pretend to bury the map at their next campsite and see who tried to dig it up.

E. Z. told Mr. Johnson about the tracks.

"He must be ridin' alone," Mr. Johnson said. "He was afeared of takin' on all of us. If he had help, they would have just attacked. I suppose he'll be trailin' us, waitin' for the right time. Keep a lookout fer him. Watch yore back."

E. Z. walked out to the middle of the Natchez Trace. Sunlight streamed through the thick tree canopies overhead and poured into a pool of light on the ground at his feet. In contrast, cage walls of dark, moss-covered trees lined the sides of the road. Beyond them, gloomy thickets hid any view that would give hope.

"It will fight you," he heard the boatman repeat in his mind. E. Z. wondered what else the mysterious road had in store for him. He was unsure he was up for the challenge.

As a cloud drifted, sunlight shone through the fog ahead to lure E. Z. further down the road, tighter into the grip of The Devil's Backbone.

CHAPTER TEN

Snakes

Everything used for the temporary campsite was packed back into the wagon. The last of the dishwater was poured to smother the campfire. Major knew the signal and performed his duty rounding up the party to leave. As the wagon pulled away along the ridgetop, the boys looked down to deeper valleys below.

David asked, "Are we in the mountains?"

"Only if you've never been in mountains," Mr. Johnson said. "The old maps show this area as mountains. The feller who drew them maps had never seen real mountains."

The word "map" gave E. Z. an opening for questions. He should have told Mr. Johnson the whole story. But he suspected that Mr. Johnson would confront Mr. Burton, and who knew where that would lead?

"What are maps good for?" E. Z. asked. "I mean, why do people draw maps?"

"That'd be obvious." Mr. Johnson said. "Either to help somebody find some place they've never been or to help somebody who's been thar remember how to find it again."

When the answer did not satisfy E. Z., Mr. Johnson added, "And sometimes a map warns what to expect in a certain area to be on the lookout and be ready."

E. Z. pressed on, "Would a map warn people about snakes?"

Mr. Johnson chuckled, "Snakes is ever'whar'. I don't see no point in makin' a map just to show that a certain place has snakes." He thought a minute and added, "Maybe, if it had a whole nest of 'em. But then, why point somebody to go to a place, just to tell him don't go thar 'cause it's full of snakes?"

E. Z. asked, "What if the snakes are guarding something, like buried treasure?"

Mr. Johnson nodded and humored the boy, "A nest of snakes would be a safe place to hide treasure. Most bandits is too lazy to fight a whole nest of snakes. Thar's easier pickin's out here for bandits—like us."

"Have you ever seen a map with snakes on it?" David asked.

Mr. Johnson shook his head, "You boys can come up with some of the wildest questions. Did you stay awake all night thinking these up just to pester me? If you did, I should have made you the camp watchmen."

E. Z. pressed on, "I saw a map with three snakes on it."

Mr. Johnson looked puzzled. "Hmm, snakes. What makes you think it was a map?"

"It had an "X" to mark a spot," E. Z. replied.

"What was at the spot?" Mr. Johnson asked.

"I don't know. Part of the map was cut off. I was just wondering whether it would be good or bad because of the snakes."

"Now, that's a deep question," Mr. Johnson pondered. "I got to admit you've stumped me. In all my years, I've never seen a map with snakes."

"Would the Natchez Trace be a good place to hide treasure?" Isaiah asked.

Mr. Johnson smiled broadly. "Hmm. Now, it *would* be like buryin' treasure in a nest of snakes. That would keep lots'a thieves from workin' hard to find it. Tell you what you do. If you ever see that map again, let me have a look at it. I'll see if I recognize the spot where the "X" is."

David and Isaiah looked at E. Z. as if they expected him to pull the map out of his boot, but he changed the subject instead. "Where do we come to next?"

"Duck River. We'll have to see how high the water is and whether we can float across it on the ferry boat, drive across it, or wait for one or t'other. If I had a flat bottom wagon, I could just take the wheels off and float across if the water is too high."

"What do we do if we have to wait a long time?" David asked.

"Oh, thar's an inn and a storehouse on this side of the river. Isaiah, you'll also be glad to know thar's a military camp thar. Maybe you'll see some soldiers. They call 'em 'rangers' 'cause they ride the road and act as scouts to look for danger."

The boys would feel safe at least one night if they were staying at a military camp. Just the mention of soldiers took Isaiah's interest. In his excitement, he talked constantly and took the boys' mind off maps, Indians, and bandits.

The road became steeper as it ran off the side of the ridge and sloped lower toward the river. The wagon turned around a small bend, and E. Z. spotted several buildings ahead. It looked like a small settlement. Several of the houses were cabins, but the two-story house with wooden siding was the inn.

When the wagon stopped, the boys and Hannah hurried to explore the site. Isaiah wanted to find the troop encampment first. He noticed the palisade wall on the hill and led the children across a small stream toward it.

"Careful," Isaiah warned them. "We don't want them to think that we are enemies. They might shoot. I am beginning to look like a soldier."

Hannah laughed, "Oh, that's silly. We don't look anything like an enemy."

E. Z. agreed, "And we don't look old enough. We should be safe."

The children walked up to the sallyport, where the earthworks wall opened to a small entrance that the soldiers easily could guard. E. Z. shouted to the sentinel to ask if they could enter. The sentinel stepped out to block the entry.

The soldier was a private, a young boy from Kentucky. The sentinel said that his company had been sent to the Natchez Trace to provide extra security for travelers. Bandits had begun attacking more settlers on the road in recent weeks.

"Have you captured any bandits?" David asked.

"No. There aren't many of us, and there are too many places for the robbers to hide along the road," the young soldier answered.

"Besides," the soldier added, "bandits look just like everybody else. They don't wear uniforms. We could pass a bandit on the road and never suspect who he was."

E. Z. thought of Mr. Burton.

Isaiah had been enthralled with this first chance to see what military life was like. He had told E. Z. that he thought soldiers spent their time every day fighting battles and saving settlers. But most of these men were chopping wood for fires, washing uniforms, and repairing buildings—the same things they did at home. The only weapon in view, besides the sentinel's musket, was a rifle that a soldier was cleaning. Isaiah tried to walk inside to get a better look, but the sentinel stopped him.

"Halt," the young soldier recited his military training manual and raised his gun. Then he resumed normal conversation, "I can't let you inside. Those are my orders."

Isaiah turned to Hannah. "See, I told you he would mistake me for a soldier."

E. Z. said, "I saw a bandit at the inn in Nashville. He died, and a man put his body on a horse, and then he disappeared."

"What did the bandit look like?" the soldier asked.

"He had a scar across his cheek, and he was missing his left ear," E. Z. replied.

"That could be a lot of people on the Natchez Trace. There are lots of fights out here. Did he have long fingernails?"

"Yes. We called them 'claws.'"

"They use those in fights if they are attacked. They gouge out eyes. What was he wearing?" the soldier asked.

"A bright coat. Cloth. It looked like a quilt," E. Z. said.

The soldier showed interest. "What color was it?"

"Orange and brown," E. Z. answered.

The sentinel's demeanor changed. "I wish our captain were here. You could talk to him, but I don't know when he is coming back. Is there anything else that you noticed? Was anyone with him?"

"Maybe another rider...but we're not sure," E. Z. answered, looking at the others to make certain they would say the same.

David interrupted, "What about..."

E. Z. glared at him. "We're not sure. An Indian man told me that the man in the coat was a 'bad man.'"

The sentinel said, "That's for sure. You're lucky that you saw him at an inn and not out on the road. That coat you saw was what one of his victims was wearing when he was attacked at Swan Creek."

The boys looked at each other to acknowledge that their suspicions that the man at the inn was a bandit had been correct.

The sentinel added, "The odd thing is that the coat was the only thing the bandit took. He had ransacked everything the man had. He must have been looking for something he didn't find."

"The map!" the boys all thought and confirmed in another glance to each other.

Hannah stopped playing with her doll and sighed in defeat as it became clear that the boys' talk of bandits had been justified. "Who did he kill?" Hannah asked.

The young sentinel answered, "No one knew his real name. But the victim made money from things he found in the Indian nations. He must have been a trader or a trapper of some kind. His mistake was that he bragged at one of the inns that he had found something in the Chickasaw Nation that would make him rich. The bandit who killed him must have heard him brag and tried to take whatever the man found once he was alone on the road."

"How do you know he didn't?" Isaiah asked.

"The bandit must have liked the man's coat and took it first. As the bandit was putting the coat on, the victim's friends came up and began firing their guns to scare the bandit off. They think the coat was all he had time to take," the sentinel said.

The sentinel saw another soldier approaching. "I'm sorry, I have told you too much already." He promised to tell the captain what the children had told him when the captain returned.

"Why aren't you out battling enemies this afternoon?" Isaiah asked the sentinel.

The sentinel laughed, "That's what I signed up for, but we spend most of our time guarding this road and waiting to be attacked."

Disappointed that they would not be able to talk with the captain, the children walked to the inn.

The store clerk told the boys where to find a fish trap, a shallow area where it would be easier to catch fish in the river. The boys pulled Mr. Johnson aside and begged him to show them how to whittle fishhooks from tree limbs.

After Mr. Johnson saw how anxious the boys were to whittle the hooks, he warned, "Now, careful not to stab yore feet with the prongs when yo're catchin' fish. We don't eat feet!"

With their prized creations, the boys ran down to the shallow area in the river to try catching fish for their dinner. Occasionally, a canoe or a small boat passed by carrying settlers who had traveled to the area to trade. The boys could not help looking across the river to the area they would be traveling the next day and wondering what waited for them there.

The fishing spot gave the boys a good position to study the military camp. David was fascinated with how the walls and earthworks were designed to make it difficult for enemies to enter it without getting shot.

"I may command that fort one day. They should've let me inspect it," Isaiah said.

"I bet if you told them about your bear-killing adventures, they would have done just that," David said.

Isaiah said, "I didn't think about those. Those stories will have to remain our secrets for now. If the fort commander heard them, he might draft me on the spot and then I wouldn't be able to help defend our traveling party."

E. Z. laughed.

The boys hoped they would catch soldiers on their return. They had better luck catching fish, and they were able to add to the summer potatoes, squash, and beans cooked for their supper that evening.

After supper, as the boys took their places on the porch for sleep, David told E. Z. he thought he heard wild animals crying out across the river. A few times, he imagined that he heard the Indian war whoops that the Nashville inn owner had described.

E. Z. noticed the sounds, too, as a heavy fog rose off the river. The fog played tricks on E. Z.'s eyes in the moonlight. He could imagine seeing Indians crossing the river in canoes in the fog.

About midnight, E. Z. jostled David to wake him. "Look!"

David brushed sleep from his eyes a couple times as if he were dreaming. "Are those Indians?" he whispered.

"I think so." E. Z. looked over and saw four men sleeping at the end of the porch that were dressed like the Indians he had seen in Nashville. In fact, they appeared to be the same men.

E. Z. pushed Isaiah to wake him. E. Z. whispered, "Indians." Isaiah's eyes opened wide. "Ind…"

"Sh… don't say anything," E. Z. whispered.

The boys quietly stood up and walked into the yard to get a better look at the Indians. The Chickasaws seemed harmless when asleep.

E. Z. said, "I don't think those Indians would be planning to scalp us if they are sleeping on the same porch as we are. And their faces are not painted for war. They must be friendly."

"Let's move our pallet off the porch and sleep somewhere else," David said.

E. Z. disagreed, "There is no place else."

"We could sleep out in the tall grass. That would be a good hiding place from the Indians," David argued.

"But not from the animals. We don't have a fire to scare them away," E. Z. said.

After speculating for more than an hour about who the Indians were and what they might be up to, the boys decided to go back to sleep on the porch.

When the boys woke, they first looked for the Indians. They were gone.

After breakfast, E. Z. searched out the storekeeper to ask about the Indians. E. Z. opened the wrong door of the storehouse and walked into a dark back room. A small group of men huddled over a stack of coins by a dim flame looked up in surprise.

"Hey, boy! You been spyin' on us? What'd you hear?" one man said. It was the man with long, stringy hair E. Z. had seen on the porch at the Nashville Inn.

The man pulled out his knife. "Come over here and let me cut yore ears off." The man laughed.

E. Z. ran out, slamming the door behind him. He could hear the other men join in with wicked laughter behind the closed door, but no one followed him outside.

E. Z. ran around the building to enter the store as he should have the first time. The storekeeper told him that Gordon's Ferry, at one time, was operated by Chickasaw chief William Colbert and "Jack" Gordon, who lived in Nashville. Gordon was a military hero to the Tennesseans. Chickasaws still felt comfortable at the inn. They slept on the porches regardless of the weather when they traveled through the area.

Now that he was fully awake, E. Z. was certain that he had recognized the Indian who had warned him in Nashville. He was disappointed that he would not be able to talk to him to learn more about the bandit. The store clerk suggested that they would likely meet the Indian man on their trip.

When E. Z. told Isaiah and David about the man with long, stringy hair, Isaiah insisted that they spy on the men and try to figure out whether they were bandits. The boys walked slowly to the back of the storehouse. The door to the room where the men gathered over a pile of gold was open, but the men were gone.

"Look! There on the floor," Isaiah said. "Is that one of the metal pieces from the body's eyes?"

E. Z. stooped down to pick it up. "No, it looks like a Spanish coin. Like the one the boat captain gave to the driver in Nashville to take us to the inn. This one is the real thing."

"Those men must have had a lot more money than they needed if they just left money laying around," David said.

"They must have known that I would come back," E. Z. said as he put the coin in the hunting bag. "I think they left it on purpose, but I don't know why."

E. Z. helped Mr. Johnson load the wagon to have the chance to talk to him alone about the men he had seen in the storeroom.

Mr. Johnson was stern. "On the Natchez Trace, never open a door unless you know what's on the other side." That is all he said about it.

CHAPTER ELEVEN

Swan Creek

———————

Once the wagon was packed and boarded, Mr. Johnson drove it down to the river. The water was too low for the ferry to operate, but low enough the wagon could drive across it.

Everyone gave an opinion on the level of the water as to whether it would be riskier to remain in the wagon or to cross the stream on foot. Mr. Johnson's opinion was the only one that mattered. The water seemed to be low enough to rise no higher than midway on the wheels.

The oxen were skittish at first, but Mr. Johnson spoke kindly to them and encouraged them to push on, "Now get along, Jim. Get along, Ole Henry. You been through higher water than this!" The oxen strained harder, and soon the wagon was again firmly on dry land.

Mr. Burton again had to give "sweet talk" to Esther. Hannah stood up in the wagon and laughed. She leaned over to Sarah. "He must have a way with women. Esther is beginning to enjoy his company. My, that was fast, wasn't it?"

Sarah smiled.

Mr. Johnson followed a winding road back up to the top of the ridge. The boys kept a watch for Indians. At times, the dirt road dipped down into the valleys where cane and other plants grew thick along the sides of the road. Mr. Johnson had to use a long knife on a pole to cut the overgrown limbs to allow them to pass.

"This wagon's a little bigger than most and them briars grow fast this time of year. Watch 'em. Don't let 'em reach in an' grab you," he said. David imagined them as hands and arms that would pull him out of the wagon.

Mr. Johnson only made it worse. "Thar was one wagon hidden along the road fer a couple months. When the driver came back fer it, the vines had covered it over. The Natchez Trace will keep you if you don't keep movin'. Don't sit in one place too long." David moved as far from the outside of the bench as he could.

E. Z. stood to twist and snap an overhanging limb. He again glimpsed a large, hairy creature crossing the road ahead. "What was that?" he asked Mr. Johnson.

"What was what?" Mr. Johnson answered.

"I thought I saw something up ahead. Something large with black fur crossed the road where the road turns up there," E. Z. said.

"Hmm. Could be a bear. I didn't see it. My eyes ain't what they used to be. I saw a feller with some spectacles in Nashville, but I don't think they would last too long on me out here."

"Aren't you worried about what kind of creature it might be?" E. Z. asked.

"Is it blockin' the road?"

"No. It kept moving."

"Then I ain't worried. If it stopped, that would mean it weren't afeared of us. Now, that's when you worry."

E. Z. did not see the creature as they passed the area where it had crossed the road.

"Has anybody ever seen a creature, an animal they couldn't identify in this area?" E. Z. asked.

"Just one. Big feller," Mr. Johnson said.

David moved over toward E. Z. until he was leaning on him.

"What does it look like?" Isaiah asked.

"Long, black fur. It's got green eyes that they say glow. That's what takes everybody's attention," Mr. Johnson said. "You'll see lots'a things you can't explain on the Natchez Trace. It's best not to think too much about 'em."

"Have you ever heard of that creature jumping on anybody's back?" E. Z. asked.

Mr. Johnson laughed. "No. It's too big. I met a feller who hunted it once. He quit when he saw that it left a paw track bigger than his huntin' dog."

"It's too big to jump?" Isaiah asked.

"No. It's so big that if it jumped on somebody's back, they wouldn't be around to tell anybody about it." Mr. Johnson looked over at Major on the buckboard floor. The dog had moved his head to hide it under the seat. "Now, we're goin' to have to change the subject. Major's no coward, but he don't like nobody talkin' about that animal or whatever it is. It gives him bad dreams. He'll keep me awake all night."

E. Z. kept an extra lookout for signs of the creature as they pushed back brush. The work of clearing limbs slowed the wagon almost to a crawl. It took much of the day to travel a few miles. Hannah kept asking when it would be time to stop.

Mr. Burton grew impatient with the slow pace. He rode ahead and then allowed the wagon to catch up at a wide spot in the road and held up his arm to flag Mr. Johnson to stop.

"I have some business I need to attend to before I leave Tennessee. I will ride ahead and meet you at the next stop. Where will that be?" Mr. Burton asked.

"Grinder's house at the Tennessee Line," Mr. Johnson said. "Now, you've heard that bandits killed a man close to here, ain't you? It don't make no sense fer you to go ridin' off alone."

"I will take my chances." Mr. Burton said. "If I was the kind of man who ran from every rumor, I would have stayed home."

"Suit yoreself," Mr. Johnson grumbled. "But we're not waitin' on you. If you go off and get yoreself shot, we'll move on without you."

Mr. Burton's face turned red. "I understand," he said slowly as he rode away.

Mr. Johnson told the boys that it was foolhardy for Mr. Burton to be riding alone past Swan Creek, with reports of bandits and all. But there was nothing he could do if Mr. Burton did not want to pay attention to the warnings. "Thar's nobody out here to save a foolish man from himself," Mr. Johnson said.

As the wagon passed by a small inn, Mr. Johnson pointed to it and said, "That's the Widow Cranfield's. She married a Chickasaw man who died several years back." Mr. Johnson explained that women owned the houses in the Indian nations.

Isaiah said, "Don't tell Hannah. She'll claim that right at home before she even gets her own house."

Mr. Johnson said that the Chickasaw man spoke little English. Whenever a traveler stopped to ask about spending the night, the old man just nodded toward his wife and grunted, "She boss."

Mr. Johnson added, laughing, "The old man was probably a ferocious Chickasaw warrior. Maybe the leader of dozens of warriors. But when he come home, 'She boss.' Now, boys, let that be a lesson to you."

The boys were not sure what the lesson was.

Limbs and brush along the road grew thick again, blocking out much of the sunlight. E. Z. understood why the road was described as "dark." Worse, odd echoes of talk mixed in with animal sounds from the woods. The trees seemed to be whispering.

David asked about whether they were getting close to the bandits.

"This area is thick with 'em," Mr. Johnson said. "Now back thar at the 'She Boss' inn, the bandit Tranium killed a man. He had a helper they never named. That man had his left ear cut off. That showed he had done it before."

E. Z. asked, "What happened to him?"

POP!

The boys jumped as if Tranium had shot at them. Mr. Johnson looked back and said something the boys did not understand. Then he said that one of the wheels had hit a stump and cracked. They would have to stop and fix it.

"Of all places to break down on the road as the sun is settin'," Mr. Johnson said. "We're not more 'n a mile of Swan Creek."

They were stranded in the middle of the bandit haven. Mr. Johnson had hoped to get beyond it before dark, but they would have to camp there for the night until he had time to repair the wheel.

The children set out to find brush to start a campfire. Because bandits were expected to be nearby, Mr. Johnson would not let the children go too far out of his sight.

As E. Z. had planned, he made a show of taking some paper from one of Sarah's trunks and walking into the woods to bury it between two rocks. He had baited the trap. He waited to see whether his "hidden treasure" attracted any of their traveling party.

Sarah and Mary fried more of Mrs. Benton's salted bacon and boiled beans they had bought at the storehouse at Gordon's Ferry. They mixed cornmeal with water to make a cornpone bread, baking it over the fire in grease from the fried bacon. Everyone seemed to have plenty to eat, and the heavy meal made everyone ready for sleep by dark.

As the boys were just drifting off, E. Z. heard a bobcat's cry close to camp. The sound came from two directions and seemed to be getting closer. E. Z. looked to make sure that the fire was burning. Mr. Stewart was camp watchman, but he had dozed off. The fire was dying down.

E. Z. listened without moving. The cry sounded like the call of the bobcat he had heard the night he saw the glistening of the band on Jack's hat. As E. Z. sat up to peer into the dark woods, he looked in the direction where he had pretended to bury the map. The familiar glistening appeared again. A lantern was being lit in the woods. As it was held up, E. Z. recognized Jack's face.

Jack had taken the bait—but it was E. Z. in the trap.

Jack waived and pointed his hand, motioning for E. Z. to follow him. E. Z. shook his head, signaling that he would not go anywhere. There was safety in numbers, and he did not want to go out alone. Jack responded by pulling out a pistol and aiming it toward Sarah, who slept on a bedroll in a small cotton tent.

Jack put his finger over his mouth to tell E. Z. not to say anything. He motioned again for E. Z. to go toward him. E. Z. arose off his pallet. David opened his eyes to see that E. Z. was leaving. David also started to rise. Isaiah turned over, still asleep.

Jack shook his head "No." He pointed to E. Z. as if to say "just you." E. Z. whispered for David to stay.

E. Z. reached for his boots but chose to put on David's boots instead. They fit poorly, and he plodded toward the woods. David started again to go with E. Z. E. Z. motioned for David to remain as he walked into the woods toward the light.

The lantern light moved quickly as if it were floating in the woods. E. Z. thought that the only one who could float was the ghost. He almost ran through the woods, barely keeping up in David's boots. The light moved so fast, in fact, that he lost a sense of what direction he was headed, and worse, how to find his way back to camp. Maybe that was Jack's intent.

The ground became slick. The sound of running water was just ahead. E. Z. was running through a shallow creek. He stopped suddenly when he noticed that the water from the creek disappeared. The water was dropping off the side of a bluff, forming a waterfall below him. He was on the side of a steep bluff, and he had nearly stepped off.

Jack motioned the lantern for E. Z. to continue to follow. E. Z. navigated along the slick creek bed with nothing to hold to keep him from falling off the side of the bluff. He had no choice but to continue, balancing himself as best he could. He kept following the light but getting farther behind.

The light stopped and floated too high in the air to be held by a man. Was the ghost with Jack? As E. Z. walked closer, he saw that the lantern had been hung from a tree limb by the opening of a cave. Something on the ground reflected the light. E. Z. stooped down to see two metal pieces that looked like ones that had covered the body's eyes at the church.

A sudden force from behind gave E. Z. a sharp shove. He fell head-first into the opening of the cave and rolled down several feet into complete darkness.

CHAPTER TWELVE

The Ghost Cave

E. Z. rubbed his head to see if it was cut. He patted his hand on the ground to discover what was around him in the dark. His hand landed on a large object, and he ran his fingers over it to figure out what it was. A human leg bone! He dropped it with disgust. E. Z. smelled his hand to see if the bone was fresh. It wasn't. He patted his hand around again and felt a skull.

The cave must be one where the bandits hid. How far down had E. Z. rolled and how would he get out? Something—maybe a small animal—brushed E. Z.'s back as it scurried deeper into the opening in the cave behind him.

A dim light appeared near the opening. E. Z. looked quickly to see whether there were any other bones. He was sitting right beside two skeletons. The room was tall enough that he could stand up. Writing on the wall of the cave was in a language different than English. Metal and wooden boxes were piled high in a corner. Maybe they were full of silver that the bandits had robbed from travelers.

The name "The Devil's Backbone" seemed appropriate for the road. E. Z. wondered what part of the Devil he was in now. He put his hand on the hunting bag to make sure he still had it. The boatman said he would need it. He did not see what good it would do.

The light brightened as it came closer. E. Z.'s heart raced as he expected to see the bandit's ghost appear where he was trapped. E. Z. was almost relieved to see Jack holding the lantern. Jack looked younger than he had from a distance. He was dirty and thin, and he smelled like he had been sleeping with pigs at one of the farms.

Jack smiled, but it wasn't a friendly smile. It was the smirk of a villain just before he attacks.

"Well, well," Jack said. "I heered tell you've been askin' lots of questions about me. And tattlin' to the rangers."

"Why have you been following us? I don't know who you are," E. Z. replied.

"This is my road," Jack said. "I like to keep up with who my *guests* are. What's yore name, anyway?"

"Ezekiel Perkins."

"I heered somebody call you somethin' like 'Easy.'"

"'E. Z.' My friends call me 'E. Z.'"

"Hmm. 'Yore *friends*?' Ain't I yore friend, E. Z.?"

"I never met you."

"I believe we had a little social call back in Nashville. Now, didn't we?"

"It wasn't a social call. You nearly ran over my brother."

Jack laughed. "He moves slow, but I'll admit he's got a good grip. And I've seen you several times since. You might have seen me a time or two. Now, ain't you?"

"I guess so." Feeling a little bolder, E. Z. asked, "What's your name?"

"You *would* like to know that, wouldn't you?" Jack continued with a fake smile, "Then, you'd have more to tattle about."

"I just…" E. Z. said.

Jack interrupted, "I'll get right to the point of our little visit. I heered tell that yore other friend has a real sharp knife. I just got my heart set on that knife, E. Z."

E. Z. stood, "He's fond of it. I doubt he would sell it."

Jack laughed hard in a high pitch. "I hadn't thought of payin' fer it. But I might." Jack looked over to the boxes and said, "I'll have to count my money first."

Jack put down the lantern and stepped toward the boxes. E. Z. slightly bent forward to reach for the lantern. Jack turned suddenly and pulled out his own knife. "I heered tell that you may have taken somethin' in Franklin that didn't belong to you." Jack walked up so close that E. Z. almost suffocated from the pig smell. "And I heered tell that whoever you took it from wants it back."

"I didn't take anything from anybody!" E. Z. said.

Jack stood silent pondering what to say next. Then he looked over E. Z.'s shoulder as if he spotted something in the dark depths of the cave behind E. Z. "Do you believe in ghosts and witches, E. Z.?"

"I don't know. I've heard stories, but to be honest, I've never seen either one."

Jack stared E. Z. straight in the eyes. "Oh, I've seen 'em. If you stay on the Natchez Trace long, you'll see 'em too. What I want to know is why would a ghost lie about you takin' somethin' from him? And at a church of all places!" Jack shook his head in pretended disappointment.

E. Z. thought of the bandit's body. But he had put the map back. He did not respond.

Jack pressed on, "He wants it back. And he's followin' you. I've seen him. Out there in the woods. He's just behind you every step. I know you've heered him. Probably felt him breathin' on the back of your neck. Admit it."

It was true that E. Z. had heard sounds in the woods behind him. But it could have been Jack or anybody. "I don't know," he said.

"That ghost might have followed you right here into this cave to that hole right behind you, and he's there waitin' on you. Is this the first time you ever been followed by a ghost, E. Z.? Do you know what ghosts can do? It ain't purty."

Jack picked up a skull and held it where it faced E. Z. "Now, just look at this feller here. Ask him what happens when a ghost traps you in a cave. Or maybe you can see fer yoreself." Jack laughed as he threw down the skull, "See. He's still too scared to talk."

Jack moved close to E. Z. again. Jack held up his knife and ran his thumb along the blade to show how sharp it was. "Well, looky there. I didn't get all the blood off from last time. Tell you what, E. Z., since I'm yore new friend, I'm goin' to do you a big favor. I'm goin' to save you from that ghost."

"How will you do that?" E. Z. wondered.

Jack said, "You just give me whatever you took, and he'll start followin' me and leave you alone. My life will be misery, that's fer sure. But I would be willin' to do that fer my new friend, E. Z. And you can repay me by keepin' your mouth shut about it."

Jack reached over to pull the hunting bag toward him to study the blood stains. "And you can go ahead and give me that huntin' bag to keep it in."

With his other hand, Jack started to raise his knife again. "Deal?"

A gunshot thundered through the cave from the outside. Jack ducked as if he were shot. He quickly sheathed his knife and fumbled to blow out the lantern. As soon as the flame was out, E. Z. heard Jack feeling the ground with his hands and moving toward the opening on his knees.

E. Z. waited. His instinct was to follow Jack and take his chances in the opening rather than the cave. Here, he was trapped with whatever had followed him inside. But a few seconds would give whoever shot the gun time to move on.

How did Jack know about the map? Who had told him? Had the bandit become a ghost? Did the bandit's ghost follow E. Z. out of the church in Franklin? Was he following him still? Was he here behind him in the cave? Was that the ghost that had brushed his back?

A puff of cold air blew from behind him deep in the cave where the ghost might be hiding. E. Z. must have been more frightened than he knew—he felt chilled. E. Z. listened for a few minutes. He heard nothing except bats fluttering into the cave and water dripping somewhere deeper behind him.

E. Z. decided he would try to escape. He put his hands down on the dirt as Jack had done and crawled on his hands and knees to follow the direction he had heard Jack leave the cave. Was it possible that the hairy, black creature he had seen also made its home in the cave? The last thing he wanted to meet in the narrow tunnel was an angry supernatural creature three times his size.

After crawling a few feet, E. Z. saw a dim light from the side. The cave made a slight turn at the opening. The ceiling of the cave near the entrance was too low to stand.

Fresh air signaled that he was nearing the entrance. Then he ran right into a pair of boots. He looked up. It was Mr. Burton!

"Ezekiel! Why have you wandered away from the others?" Mr. Burton asked as he extended a hand to help E. Z. to his feet.

E. Z. gave a partial answer, "I thought I saw someone in the woods. And I followed him here."

Mr. Burton frowned. "I am not your father, and it is not my place to tell you what to do, but walking out here in the dark by yourself was foolish. I thought I saw someone too. I fired my pistol to scare him off."

E. Z. knew that Mr. Burton could not have seen Jack when he fired the shot. Jack had been in the cave. Maybe he had seen the bandit's ghost near the opening of the cave. Maybe the ghost was following him as Jack had said. Or maybe it had been the creature. E. Z. instinctively put his hand on the goosebumps on the back of his neck as he again felt a chill.

"Come along. Let's get you back to the others." Mr. Burton stopped and looked at E. Z. "This is not a safe area. Whoever I scared off might still be around. Are you carrying any valuables that I should safeguard until we are back?" Mr. Burton asked.

"No. I didn't even have time to bring my knife. I am carrying nothing a bandit would want," E. Z. said, relieved that he had left the map behind.

Mr. Burton was probably a good card player and gambler, but his face did not hide his disappointment as they rode Esther back to camp.

As E. Z. dismounted the horse, Mr. Johnson met him. "Are you alright, boy?"

"Yess'r. I'm fine."

Captain Stark was next. "We heard the shot. When we couldn't find you, your mother was beside herself. You shouldn't worry her like that, Ezekiel."

Sarah ran out of her tent and hugged E. Z. tight. Then she scolded him. "It was dangerous running off. You could have got yourself killed."

Sarah had no idea how close they both had come to being killed. Maybe it was time for E. Z. to tell his mother what he knew. He would not have a chance to talk to her without being overheard until morning. He whispered that he would tell her all about it as soon as they had passed Swan Creek and could talk alone. She had to trust him until then.

Sarah looked into E. Z.'s eyes. He had never given his mother reason to doubt him. He had always told her the truth as far as she knew. She agreed they would wait until they had traveled down the road.

Isaiah gave E. Z. a pat on the back. David hugged his brother. The boys wanted to hear all about Jack, but everyone in camp could hear their conversation. E. Z. told Mr. Johnson that the boys were going to visit the privy.

"Thar's no privy for miles," Mr. Johnson said.

"Ma won't let me say the other word." E. Z. said as the boys stepped into the woods away from camp. E. Z. gave them a quick summary.

"I know you told me to stay," David said, "And I did at first, but I couldn't. I woke up Isaiah."

"We tried to find you, but we didn't want to get too far from camp, and you had disappeared. We were going to give you another few minutes to return before we woke everybody, and then we heard the shot. Everybody woke up then," Isaiah said.

"Do you think he will come back?" David asked.

"I don't think he ever left. I think he has followed us the whole time," E. Z. said.

"Has the ghost followed us too?" David asked.

"I don't know. Mr. Burton said he saw someone outside the cave. I saw those two metal pieces again at the cave. It may have been the ghost. I'll talk to Mr. Johnson about it tomorrow. Let's get some sleep. It won't be long until sunup."

"I won't sleep if the ghost is here. Why is he tormenting us?" David asked.

"It's not just a ghost," E. Z. said, "It's this road. The boatman said it would fight us. We'll see what it has in store for us tomorrow."

CHAPTER THIRTEEN

The Spaniard

The sun seemed to rise earlier the next morning because they had all gotten little sleep. It was even more difficult to wake up because a heavy fog hung close to the ground and shielded much of its light. It would be easy for anyone to follow them close in the fog and not be seen.

Mr. Johnson rose first to finish temporary repairs to the wagon wheel. He woke E. Z. and asked him to help. E. Z. soon realized that Mr. Johnson could have fixed the wheel on his own. He wanted to teach E. Z. how it was done. Mr. Johnson needed an iron forge to make the wheel as good as new, but that repair would have to wait.

Mr. Johnson took his place in the driver's seat. Major recognized that action as a signal to begin barking to round up everyone to board the wagon.

They had not traveled far when the wagon came to a stop. Mr. Johnson again told everyone to get out—this time to go down a steep hill. They had arrived at the notorious Swan Valley, but the heavy morning fog hid it below.

Mr. Johnson talked quieter than usual, "Now folks, stay as quiet as possible. We're close to the caves whar them bandits hide out. The last thing we need is to draw thar attention." Major lay down low on the buckboard and put his head between his paws as if he were hiding.

Mr. Johnson continued, "When you git to the bottom of the hill, thar's a heavy cane break on both sides." He said that cane breaks were places where tall cane plants grew so thick that bandits or Indians could hide and never be seen. E. Z. wondered whether the hairy creatures hid out there too. It sounded like a good hiding place for them.

Mr. Johnson continued, "Now, directly, we'll come up to Captain Dobbins' inn and a small settlement. Usually, I'd stop at the first inn to use its forge to fix the wheel. But, somethin' tells me it's not safe this time. So, when I stop at the edge of the cane break, everybody git back in the wagon without sayin' a word. Understand?"

The boys nodded in agreement. But they felt as if Mr. Johnson were abandoning them as they saw the wagon descend the hill. He left them alone to follow it into the fog.

Sarah walked forward to take E. Z.'s and David's hands. At first, E. Z. pulled away, thinking that he was too old to have his mother hold his hand. But then it became clear that Sarah was seeking assurance that their family would defend themselves as a group. He took her hand and reached for David's.

Mr. Stewart picked Hannah up to carry her. The captain reached for his rifle and then walked in front of his family to guard them. When the old soldier saw Sarah and her sons walking in front, he moved to the head of the line to be the first to face any threat. Mr. Burton rode Esther up to the lead to join them.

It seemed too quiet. All they could hear was the cawing of a lone crow in the distance. David barely breathed as he tried to see into the cane break. E. Z. knew what his brother was thinking—Indian warriors were good at keeping quiet and blending into the woods. E. Z. tried to imagine himself as the Indian boy in training to become a warrior. What would an animal look for?

Hundreds of blackbirds appeared from nowhere. Their deafening flutters filled the eerie silence as they flew inches above the travelers' heads. Just as suddenly, the birds disappeared into the fog. Something nearby had scared them. E. Z. tried to listen as an Indian warrior might. He heard nothing different.

Whatever was just out of sight chose not to attack. Mr. Johnson would say that they had passed through too early for the worst bandits to be awake. They normally caroused through the night. The wagon stopped at the base of the hill as Mr. Johnson promised, and everyone took his place.

As the wagon passed by Dobbins' Stand, several men came out of the inn to check on their horses tied at the front. One old man tipped his hat, but the others stared at the wagon as if they were sizing up what it carried. E. Z. thought one man was staring at the hunting bag, but he convinced himself that it was his imagination.

"Don't stare back at him," Mr. Johnson said low. "Don't give him any idea you know what he's thinkin'." E. Z. hoped that the men were headed in the opposite direction.

At the bottom of the valley, Swan Creek was shallow and cool. Any other time in the summer, the wagon might have stopped for the children to take a morning swim that would serve as a rare bath. But they could not risk the danger of halting.

Mr. Johnson told the boys that Chickasaws bathed every day.

"Even in winter?" David asked.

"Yep. They break the ice to reach the water if they have to."

"Why would they do that?" Isaiah asked.

"You'd have to ask them why. Don't sound too civilized to me," Mr. Johnson said.

None of the boys could imagine taking a bath when it was not necessary.

The next rise to the ridge was gradual enough that everyone could remain seated. As they reached the top, they rose above the fog as if they were birds rising above the clouds.

Even the deer were late rising for the morning, and they stood by the road grazing on tall grass. E. Z. wondered whether the bandits had been so active in the area that they kept the deer from sleeping too.

After the party moved beyond the valley where Swan Creek ran, Mr. Johnson quizzed E. Z. about where he had gone the night before. E. Z. told him about the cave and the skeleton. E. Z. still was reluctant to tell more about the map. Then, he mentioned that Mr. Burton had found him at the cave entrance.

"I didn't know whar he found you. What business did he have thar at that time of night?" Mr. Johnson asked.

"I guess he was saving me from bandits," E. Z. said.

Mr. Johnson was silent.

"The boy I saw in the woods at our first stop is still trailing us. I call him 'Jack.' That's who I saw last night. I followed him." E. Z. left out the part about Jack threatening to kill Sarah. He did not want Jack to think he was "tattling" to get him into trouble and then go through with his threat.

"What did he look like?" Mr. Johnson asked.

"Not a lot older than me. Real thin. Smelled like pigs."

Mr. Johnson frowned. "How do you know what he smelled like?"

"I got downwind of him."

Mr. Johnson laughed, remembering that he told E. Z. to stay upwind of his spitting.

E. Z. noticed that Mr. Johnson did not seem surprised that Jack was following them. He saw Mr. Johnson feel the pocket of his coat for his firearm to make sure it was there.

"Did you find out that anybody else was followin' us?" Mr. Johnson asked.

"Maybe a ghost," E. Z. said.

"A ghost?" Mr. Johnson said with pretended seriousness. "What makes you think a ghost is followin' us?"

"Jack told me," is all E. Z. chose to reveal.

Mr. Johnson smiled. "Hmm. Tell you what you do. You let me take care of that young feller Jack if he shows up and you boys take care of the ghost."

"How would we do that?" E. Z. asked.

Mr. Johnson said, "If you pester it with as many questions as you throw out to me every day, it'll high tail it outta here in no time."

The boys held their questions for a while. They did not want Mr. Johnson to leave them out there in the woods.

Within the hour, the wagon crossed a second Swan Creek, Little Swan Creek, and then began a slow pull up to the top of another hill. The boys could see wagon tracks beside the road where other wagons had gotten stuck in wet weather. Mr. Johnson told them that when the road became too bad in one spot for the wheels to move, travelers just moved over and created a new path with their wagons.

"Let that be another lesson, boys. Them settlers don't let nothin' stand in thar way. Out here, yo're goin' to face lots'a obstacles like that muddy area back thar. You just got to figure out a better way around 'em," he said. "You got to be smarter and stronger than whatever runs up again' you." It was the same advice Mrs. Benton had given.

The wagon circled around the top of the ridge. The boys spotted Grinder's house and stables ahead. They had arrived early in the day for a stop. But Mr. Johnson said that Grinder's was the last house in the settled part of the country before they reached the lower Mississippi area. They would stop there for a day, rest, and buy whatever provisions they needed before continuing. He could also use their forge to fix the wagon wheel.

As the children explored the yard, Mr. Johnson pointed out a small rise a few feet south of the house. It was a shed—not a building but a watershed. Water on the north side of that point ran all the way north to the Duck River where they had crossed at Gordon's Ferry. Water on the other side ran south to the Buffalo River. He pointed west across the road, and he said that the road was the eastern boundary of the Chickasaw Nation. He pointed to the south. That, he said, was the northern border of the Chickasaw Nation.

They were on the edge of Indian territory, and they could expect to see more Indians from that point on. He reminded the children to be on their best behavior and not to have much to do with the Indians. The Indians might misunderstand some of their actions and attack.

David stood at the watershed, obviously intrigued by the thought that a drop of water at one spot would drain all the way to a river.

Isaiah opened a canteen and poured out some water on the ground.

"What did you do that for?" David asked.

Isaiah joked, "I might be thirsty when we get to the river. This water will be waiting for me. I get first chance at whatever water we find there. That will be mine."

"Don't plant that seed in his mind. He'll be up all night drawing it on his tablet," E. Z. warned.

Sarah put her hand on E. Z.'s arm to pull him aside from the others. She said that it was time to take a walk. The man who worked in the stables had told her that there was a large, gushing spring just east of the house."

Sarah and E. Z. made a pretense of carrying a water bucket to the spring to get water to wash E. Z.'s shirt. Mr. Johnson called out, "Ezekiel, come talk to me after supper tonight. I got some information fer you about them 'snakes' you asked me about."

E. Z. nodded in agreement to meet him. Sarah said, "I hate snakes. Watch out for them as we walk through this brush."

As E. Z. and Sarah walked down the hill to the spring, E. Z. told his mother the story, except for the part of Jack pointing the pistol at her. He still did not want to scare her.

"We have to tell someone," she said.

"There's no one here we can tell." E. Z. said. "I told one of the soldiers at Gordon's Ferry, but it did no good. We're on our own now."

"We can tell the men in our party. We can depend on each other for safety," she added.

"Can we? How do we know who we can trust? We just met these people a few days ago. Remember, the bandits sometimes meet up with people traveling on the road and pretend to be their friends."

"But we know everyone by now," Sarah said.

"We don't know why Mr. Burton was at the cave last night or where Mr. Stewart goes when we stop at the springs."

Sarah's eyes again showed a hint of fear. E. Z. wanted his mother to know that she had taken false comfort from the conversations in the wagon and around the campfire. They did not know anything about their traveling companions other than what their companions wanted them to know.

E. Z. said, "Suppose this map is valuable. Or that Isaiah's knife is more than just a knife. Do we know that one of the people with us won't be tempted to rob us for them?"

Sarah said, "I suppose I have become too trusting. I just knew that I needed friends out here. But I see why people travel with others they know."

E. Z. added, "Now we don't have any choice. We could turn and go back, but we're at least three days from Nashville. We would be going through some dangerous area on our own, especially if bandits are following us. They would pick us off for sure."

Sarah's shoulders trembled and tears fell down her cheeks. E. Z. put his arm around his mother and gave her a hug. "Don't worry, Ma. You've got David and me. You can trust us. Together, we are the man of the family."

Sarah smiled. "Yes, I do have you, and I am very proud of you both." She wiped her eyes. "What was I thinking?" She gave E. Z. a hug. "I feel foolish. Here I am worried about a child bandit and a 'ghost' following us, and out there," she said pointing south," we have a big farm waiting for us. How much work we must do before winter! That is what we should be thinking about."

E. Z. asked, "What do we do with the map?"

Sarah thought a minute and answered, "You did the right thing by not taking the real one. It was not yours. I suppose it will not do any harm to keep the copy. If it leads you to something that does not belong to somebody else, you can decide what to do with whatever you find then."

E. Z. smiled. "I'm glad I could finally tell you. I thought I was going to bust keeping it to myself."

They filled the cedar bucket with water from the spring and walked back up the hill to Grinder's. Sarah took E. Z.'s shirt to boil in the water, adding some urine that the women kept in a bottle as bleach to take out stains.

Grinder's Stand did not have the storehouse and military camp like the one they had seen at Gordon's Ferry. There was a small common room with a hearth in the corner. Mrs. Grinder offered a meal at a price. But the women insisted that they eat food left over from breakfast to save money.

Sarah looked at her friends with a new suspicion at supper. She talked less about her own experiences and began listening more to the party talk about theirs.

As the travelers were finishing supper, Mr. Burton announced that he was going for a walk. Mr. Stewart waited a few minutes then followed him. The sun was setting, but neither man took a lantern. E. Z. excused himself to follow them both. Isaiah distracted him with a joke, and by the time he got outside, both were already out of sight.

E. Z. searched for Mr. Johnson to learn what he had discovered about the map. When E. Z. could not find him in the yard around the inn, he went to the stables. Mr. Johnson had repaired the wagon wheel. The forge outside was still hot. E. Z. called his name. But only crickets answered.

A deep grunt sounded from the woods behind the stables.

E. Z. walked slowly to the edge of the woods. "Mr. Johnson? Are you alright?" E. Z. yelled.

A narrow trail led to the direction of the sound. E. Z. hesitated. He could not see far into the darkening woods. The grunt sounded louder. E. Z. did not want to go into the woods alone, but he could not take the chance that Mr. Johnson was injured. E. Z. slowly inched toward the sound.

Twigs snapped ahead as the grunt sounded again. E. Z. made a short turn on the trail, and then he froze. A sharp, pungent odor hit him. A wall of black fur was all he could see. "The creature!" was all he could think. The grunt sounded again. Slowly, the animal turned and faced E. Z.

E. Z. stared the animal straight in the eyes. He breathed some relief that the eyes were not green, as Mr. Johnson had described the creature's green eyes. This animal was a bear.

E. Z. stood his ground out of fear rather than courage. His feet would not move.

The bear studied E. Z., then turned its head and slowly walked away. E. Z. remembered Mr. Johnson's advice that if the animal moved, it was not a threat. He exhaled and realized that he had been holding his breath. Though E. Z. wanted to run back to the safety of the inn, he walked forward to the spot where the bear had been standing to make sure that Mr. Johnson was not there.

E. Z. ran back to the inn and excitedly reported seeing the bear.

Sarah and Mary were alarmed, but Mrs. Grinder laughed, "We see that ole bear all the time. He may have followed you for miles if he smelled the food in your wagon."

E. Z. said, "But Mr. Johnson is missing. Do you think the bear attacked him?"

Mrs. Grinder said, "That bear ain't killed nobody yet. Son, if you're goin' to live on the Natchez Trace, you'd better get used to seein' bears."

The women assured the boys that Mr. Johnson would not abandon them. He had probably walked into the woods to take some of his liquid corn supper.

Mr. Burton and Mr. Stewart returned separately. When told that Mr. Johnson was missing, both vowed they had not seen him anywhere.

Three strangers entered the common room and asked to spend the evening at the inn. The men wore light, linen shirts and pants in the summer heat. They could afford to buy their dinner from Mrs. Grinder. The boys stared at the men as they ate hot food cooked in the kitchen cabin behind the common room. It smelled delicious.

When the strangers had finished eating, they took cane-bottom chairs outside and sat in the cool breeze from a thunderstorm just south. Lightning flashed constantly in the sky over the Indian land where the party was headed. Thunder shook the ground with its rolling rumbles.

The boys brought blankets to sit near the men and try to learn more about them. The strangers smoked long clay pipes and talked as if the boys were not there. It became clear that the men were following someone they never named. One man spoke with a foreign accent that E. Z. recognized as Spanish. He once saw a Spaniard who traveled through Pennsylvania selling leather.

The Spaniard's friend revealed more than he realized. "I hear that map is worth its weight in gold, if you know what I mean."

The Spaniard said, "A map weighs nothing. But that map *is very* heavy to carry. Is it worth it?"

The other stranger took a long puff on his pipe and said, "As long as you are not the one carrying it."

The strangers laughed.

Mention of the map took the boys' attention. David began to stare. When the Spaniard noticed David was listening to their talk, he changed the subject. "I have heard that travelers have been killed near this house. They say that there is a bandit who spends time here. He robs and kills travelers who have money. I do not know his name."

The boys had seen no one else. Jack was either gone or staying out of sight.

Isaiah whispered, "Mr. Johnson should know about the bandit who stays at Grinder's. Let's see if he is back."

The boys found a lantern to take to the stables. E. Z. carried a large stick in case the bear returned. Isaiah made sure to find a larger stick.

E. Z. remembered Mr. Johnson's advice not to open a door unless he knew what was on the other side. He opened the stables door inch-by-inch and looked inside. Jim and Ole Henry were there with the other oxen where they belonged. "Mr. Johnson. Are you asleep?" Isaiah called out. There was no answer.

E. Z. said, "I will check this side. Isaiah you check the other side."

It was unusual for Mr. Johnson to stay away from the party. They were his responsibility. The silence emphasized that he was still gone. It was so quiet, E. Z. sensed that Mr. Johnson was not coming back.

When E. Z. walked into the back pen, lightning from the storm crashed in the woods nearby, and he heard a sound above him. As he looked up, a body fell from the loft above and pushed him into the hay.

E. Z. flailed his arms to push the body off. David rushed in to see what had happened. When E. Z. turned to see whose body it was, he saw Isaiah. Isaiah began to laugh, "You thought the bandit had got you."

"That's not funny," E. Z. said as he jumped on Isaiah and wrestled him in the hay.

"When you two are through playing, can we go back to the inn?" David asked.

E. Z. stood up and brushed hay off his shirt. "I wonder if Mr. Johnson tried to take care of Jack like he promised." E. Z. said.

"We could have just given Jack the map to keep Mr. Johnson," David suggested.

"Look for the painted pieces we saw on the body's eyes," E. Z. said. As Isaiah moved the lantern behind the stables, light glistened from two spots.

David pointed. "There they are." He refused to touch them.

E. Z. said, "They don't prove the bandit's ghost was here. But we keep finding them along the road where things happen. We had better tell someone that Mr. Johnson is missing."

The boys had trouble falling asleep on Grinder's porch that night. They listened for every sound from the woods, expecting to hear Mr. Johnson's booming voice. In its place were only sounds of cicadas and wild animal movements that were common to a summer night in the Southwest.

Once, E. Z. saw a familiar glistening in the woods that he suspected was from the band in Jack's hat, but he could not be certain. When E. Z. dozed off, he dreamed that he saw the lantern floating in the air, and he followed it out to the woods to Mr. Johnson's body. The painted metal pieces covered his eyes. E. Z. awoke suddenly in a cold sweat and stayed awake with the other boys.

David interrupted their studied listening, "What if they've killed Mr. Johnson, and he's a ghost?"

"That's a terrible thing to think. He's only been gone a few hours," E. Z. said, still seeing Mr. Johnson's body in his mind.

"If he is a ghost, do you think he is a good ghost or a bad ghost?" David continued.

"He would have to be a good ghost. And he would be mad at being killed and leaving us all behind," E. Z. said.

"Do you think his ghost will fight the ghost of the bandit?" David asked.

"I don't know why he wouldn't. He might even take on Jack while he's at it," E. Z. said.

"I'd like to see that," Isaiah said. He stood up and acted out actions of a floating ghost fighting attackers.

E. Z. said, "We shouldn't even be talking like this. Go to sleep. Maybe Mr. Johnson will be back for breakfast in the morning."

But Mr. Johnson did not appear for breakfast either. The party followed their routine preparations to travel, somehow expecting Mr. Johnson to appear from the woods.

As they gathered their things to load the wagon, no one talked. Normally, by that point, Major began barking and....

"Major!" E. Z. said. "Major is missing too!"

The adults discussed their options. If they remained more than a day or two at Grinder's, they would begin to run out of food and then money. They either had to spend most of their funds waiting for Mr. Johnson at Grinder's or press on to the Mississippi Territory without him. Returning home was not an option.

The boys had lost a friend. Two, if they counted Major. E. Z. realized that it was more than that. Mr. Johnson had given them the advice that their father would have given if he were still alive. The trip would not seem the same. Who could they talk to that they could trust?

Captain Stark stepped forward and said, "A good soldier is always prepared. I have driven a few wagons in my day. I am not familiar with the Natchez Trace, but I am willing to drive the wagon."

"I don't see that we have any choice," Mr. Stewart said.

The party discussed their dilemma and voted to let Captain Stark become the driver and move on toward the Mississippi Territory.

One of the men dressed in white linen said that his party would be riding north. He promised to tell the rangers at Gordon's Ferry that Mr. Johnson had gone missing.

His Spaniard friend walked over to E. Z. when he noticed E. Z.'s hunting bag. "I did not see that bag in the dark last night. Where did you get it?"

"A boatman gave it to me. Mr. Burton thinks it belonged to a soldier," E. Z. said.

Without asking, the Spaniard reached out to hold the bag close to examine the design. "Not army, I think." He pulled up the flap and felt the thickness of the hide. A puzzled look on the Spaniard's face turned to surprise.

"How much will you take for it?" the Spaniard asked.

E. Z. said, "I can't sell it. I don't know why, but I have to carry this with us."

Mr. Burton saw the man talking with E. Z. and he walked up to stand behind him. "Is everything alright?"

The Spaniard turned and returned to the inn without speaking.

"You have to be careful here, Ezekiel. You should trust no one until you get to know him," Mr. Burton said.

"Funny, that's just what I tell Ma," E. Z. replied as he stared at Mr. Burton.

Mr. Burton dropped his head and walked away to prepare Esther for the ride.

CHAPTER FOURTEEN

The Baron

Captain Stark welcomed the boys to take their places on the wagon driver's seat. He said that he needed their help now that they were trained navigators. But E. Z. knew the real reason. Putting the boys in the back of the wagon would make it more obvious that everything had changed without Mr. Johnson.

The captain managed a chuckle. "Ezekiel, I believe that it's time to distribute rations of our candy supply to the troops."

E. Z. reached into the hunting bag and pulled out five pieces. He offered one to the captain, but he refused. He distributed the rest to each child. He instinctively reached down to hand the remaining one to Major. The dog's spot looked empty.

The oxen were unwilling to cooperate at first. The captain pulled at the reins, but it only seemed to make the animals mad. They refused to move.

"What are the leaders' names, again?" the captain asked.

"Jim and Ole' Henry," E. Z. said.

"Alright, Jim and Ole Henry, let's see what you can do," the captain said as he pulled again. The oxen only snorted and stubbornly lifted up their front hooves and planted them in the dirt. They stood still. Ole Henry turned his head and looked back at the captain with a puzzled look in his eyes.

"That's not how Mr. Johnson does it," said E. Z.

"No? Then, why don't you show me how it's done."

"Now, get along Jim. Get along Ole Henry….," E. Z. mimicked Mr. Johnson's song to the oxen. "Ma, wouldn't want me to repeat the rest of it."

The captain laughed. "Well, that much seems to be working. They're listening to you," he said as the oxen stepped forward.

The captain turned the wagon south and crossed over the boundary into the Chickasaw Nation. It seemed even more mysterious without their experienced guide. No one spoke for almost an hour.

Captain Stark broke the silence. "Have I ever told you about the time I drove a wagon for General Washington?" Isaiah and David snapped out of their depression to hear all about it.

Mr. Burton looked restless. He kept riding too far ahead, often out of the captain's sight. The captain was still not familiar with the wagon or the oxen and he did not want to drive them too fast. Captain Stark blew Mr. Johnson's tin horn to get Mr. Burton's attention to slow down. It did no good. Eventually, Mr. Burton rode completely out of sight.

E. Z. had expected Indian land to be different. But it looked just like the other parts of Tennessee that he had seen. Except that there were no settler houses.

It was some comfort, then, when E. Z. spotted an inn ahead. This, he would learn, was a Chickasaw inn.

Captain Stewart decided that it was best to stop the wagon at the inn and get information about the "lay of the land." He said that he needed to know what to expect just ahead.

Isaiah tugged at E. Z.'s shirt. "Do you want to fight a quick battle?"

"We had better not. We're in Indian territory now. Mr. Johnson said that we shouldn't do anything to make the Indians think we are attacking," E. Z. said.

When Mr. Johnson had been leading the party, the boys felt that he was watching out for dangers. Without him, E. Z. bore more responsibility to learn about where they were and where they were headed. His family was in a dangerous area relying on strangers.

Captain Stark appeared trustworthy and good-intentioned, but he was an old man. And he knew little more than E. Z. about where he was. What the captain had learned from his days in the army was how to use his skills to survive wherever he was and whatever happened. E. Z. determined to learn more of those skills from the captain.

The inn was called "McLish's." The name struck E. Z. as odd for an Indian's. But it was operated by a man whose father was a settler from Scotland. He had moved to the Chickasaw Nation and married a Chickasaw woman.

Not far from the inn, there was a pit where enslaved black men dug for iron ore. Others operated a forge where they shaped the iron into products settlers could use, such as horseshoes, pots, and plows. The forge seemed out of place with what E. Z. expected to see in an Indian nation.

"This is where the Indians made the pots they'll boil us in," Isaiah joked.

Captain Stark frowned at the joke. "Isaiah, leave Ezekiel and me to more serious business." The captain nudged E. Z. toward the inn. Its store was so large that settlers traveled good distances to trade there.

As the captain and E. Z. entered the inn, a post rider rode in from Nashville. The post rider introduced himself as "John Donley." He was traveling south like the Johnson party. He worked with Mr. Swaney under a government contract to deliver the mail.

Donley said that he knew Mr. Johnson. The men who had been at Grinder's house had told him about Mr. Johnson's disappearance. The men had assured him that they would inform the rangers.

Donley tried to reassure E. Z. "People disappear on the Natchez Trace. Sometimes, against their will. But sometimes, they turn up. I would wager that you will see Johnson again."

"In this life, I hope," Captain Stark said.

"Johnson's a tough old bird. And cantankerous as a nest of hornets. If somebody took him, they'll be wanting to give him back by now," Donley said.

It was encouraging that one of the men who rode the Natchez Trace like Mr. Johnson still had hope. E. Z. asked Donley, "Will you join our party and go along with us? We are headed the same direction, and you know where we are going."

Donley shook his head. "I am sorry, son. It's not allowed. Post riders have a schedule to meet. One man on a horse can travel more than twice as fast as a wagon loaded with people."

"Where's the next inn?" the captain asked.

Donley said, "Young Factor's, a little over 20 miles south. Another day's ride for you. It's a fine inn. You'll find whatever you need there.

"How far is it to the Tennessee River?" the captain asked.

"About three days ahead. The Chickasaw chief George Colbert operates the ferry boat to cross the river to the south bank. Once you are across on the south side, you'll see that Colbert has an inn and a small settlement. He will take good care of you. One warning though."

"What's that?" the captain asked.

"Plan your ride to arrive there before dark. If you get there too late, Colbert won't send any men out to pull you across 'til the next day. It's not safe for his men to be on the river after dark. Bandits know that, and they camp out on the north riverbank like seagulls waiting for fish to wash up on shore so they can feed on them. You would make a good target."

"We appreciate the warning," Captain Stark said, tipping his hat.

"If I see Johnson, I'll give him a razzin' for leaving his wagon and his party stranded. Then, once I have him stirred up like a mad hornet, I'll send him your way." Donley swapped mail with the clerk at the inn and rode off.

"I think we should make camp here for the night until we get a better idea of where we are headed," the captain said.

"But we've only gone three miles. We need to cover more territory every day so we don't run out of food or money," E. Z. added. They were still within riding distance of Swan Creek caves and their bandits.

The captain disagreed. "We need a plan. We are traveling blind, and we could find ourselves stopping at the wrong place at the wrong time. 'Consider your steps where they lead,'" the captain quoted from *Ecclesiastes*, a little off point. "It sounds like Young Factor's Inn is a full-day's ride. We need to plan our supplies and get whatever we need here."

E. Z. was anxious to move beyond Jack's territory to avoid another visit from the traveling pig sty.

"The letter that we left for Johnson said that we would stop at the next inn. Let's give him time to find us," the captain said.

It would also give Jack plenty of time to catch up, but E. Z. saw little choice. "Alright, Captain. What can we do to make our plan?"

"Let's talk with some of the people here and try to make a general map of where we are headed. Next, we can figure out how long it will take to get there—allowing a day or two for unexpected events—and then, we should make a list of what we will need."

It seemed logical when the captain said it. "Why did we not make this plan at Grinder's before we left?" E. Z. asked.

The captain said, "We should have done just that. My age is catching up with me. There are other men in this unit, but none that I trust to keep us organized. Young Ezekiel, if you will serve as my aide-de-camp, the party should arrive just fine."

It was a responsibility that E. Z. had not planned to shoulder. In fact, E. Z. suddenly realized that he had not appreciated how serious this journey was for his family. He had thought of himself still as a child on an adventure. His mother had said so when she told him about the trip. But he would soon be responsible for helping build a new home and a farm. It would be up to him to run it—and to defend it.

E. Z. would not shy away from the challenge. His mother and David depended on him.

E. Z. studied the people seated at tables in the common room at the inn. Most appeared rough. A group of sunburned men talked about floating down the Mississippi River and walking back up the Natchez Trace. The smallest man in that group stared at everyone as if he expected a fight to break out. A group of traders at another table included a nervous man who looked willing to give the small man the fight he was expecting.

Everyone avoided a large man with an "HT" branded on his forehead. Someone said that the "HT" stood for "horse thief." He must have been convicted and the brand was his punishment. He sat alone and drank more than anyone else.

E. Z. kept his voice low, "Captain, we should not let too many people know that we don't have a guide. Bandits could take advantage of us."

"I agree. Let's separate friend from enemy before reaching out," the captain said. He began surveying the room.

The captain said, "Ah, look at that gentleman over there." He pointed to a large, portly, well-dressed man seated at a table. The man's full attention was focused on helping himself to a large helping of Chickasaw beef. "He appears as if he has done well living off the land. He should be able to give us good information."

Without giving E. Z. time to object, the captain walked over to the man and extended his hand for a handshake. The man was using both hands to stuff as much beef into his mouth as it would hold. He glanced up, annoyed that the captain would want to shake his hand as he was eating.

"Sir, you will excuse me from extending a hand," the man said with a mouthful, spitting pieces as he spoke.

Captain Stark apologized and asked to join the man. The captain introduced himself and E. Z., giving special emphasis to his service in the army to build the man's trust. The man waived for the two to join him.

"I hate to impose on you, Sir, but we have lost our driver. He knew where he was going and we are a little lost," the captain said.

"Lost sheep," the man said between bites, adding below his breath, "Beware of wolves."

The old captain heard him, "Oh, we have met a few wolves. They seem to be attracted to this road."

"Indeed, they are." The man took nearly a full minute to finish chewing. "If you are recruiting a new driver, I am not your man."

The captain said, "No, we need information about what lies ahead—where we can find the inns along the way and land in the Mississippi Territory."

The man stopped chewing, but his eyes still looked hungry. "Land?"

"Yes," the captain said. "Our party is traveling south to buy land for farms."

"Do you have money to buy land?" the man asked.

"We would not be making this journey if we didn't. We have heard that we can buy large tracts cheap in the Mississippi Territory," the captain said.

"Well, why didn't you say so? I *can* help you," the man said. He wiped off his greasy hands and extended his right hand to the captain and his left to E. Z. But E. Z. waited to shake the right hand the proper way.

"Forgive me for not introducing myself. I am Baron Wilhelm von Strauss. I do not tell just anyone my heritage. I usually say that 'Baron' is my given name."

"Baron?" the captain asked. "You are from European royalty?"

"Well," the Baron laughed a little unconvincingly, "that makes little difference now. Since the Revolution, we all have the same opportunities."

"Spoken like a true Jefferson Democratic-Republican," the captain said. And looking at E. Z., he chuckled, "I trust him already."

E. Z. stared at the grease on the Baron's chin and stains on his shirt and wondered what a baron would be doing in the Chickasaw Nation.

The Baron sensed E. Z.'s doubts by looking at his eyes and he quickly addressed his concern. "Go on to the Mississippi Territory if you like. There is cheap land there. And it will remain cheap for as long as the Indians maintain their claims to this land."

"Why is that?" the captain asked, a little deflated.

"It is simple. You are an army man. I ask you. How do you defend the Lower Mississippi land? You cannot. If the British decide to invade from the coast, who will stop them? Much of the regular army and the militia of any size are located north of the Indians. The army would never have time to march south to stop them."

"That is true," the captain agreed.

"Or if the Creek Indians or another southern tribe decides to make war on a settlement, they would wipe it out before the army or a large militia arrives to defend it."

"I hadn't considered that. So then why are so many people moving southwest to the Mississippi Territory?" the captain asked.

"Because they do not have your military training. Even if someone told them, they would not understand these things. Now, who did you serve under?" the Baron asked.

"I had the honor of serving under General Washington," the captain bragged.

"General Washington! Well, Sir, the honor is all mine," the Baron stood and bowed to the captain.

The captain was flattered. E. Z. thought that the Baron made too much of a show of his recognition for the captain. The Baron pulled his chair closer to the captain's and began talking in a lower tone. "I am sure that General Washington could trust you with government secrets."

"Yes," the captain said, beginning a story of carrying a message during the war, "Once he handed me..."

The Baron interrupted him. "Because you served under General Washington, I know that I can trust *you* with government secrets."

"On my life," the old captain assured. "I will always be in service to my country."

"It is fortunate that you sought me out here today. I can confide in you that there are better opportunities for land not far from here. The values will rise much faster," the Baron said.

"Here?" the captain asked.

"Tell me, were you surprised to find such a large mining operation here in the Chickasaw Nation?" the Baron asked.

"We were both surprised," E. Z. said.

"Now, look over there behind that counter," the Baron said pointing toward a closet with a half-door with bars over it in the corner. "Do you recognize that stand as an official U.S. government post office?"

"Yes. In fact, I talked with the post rider Donley when we walked in," the captain answered.

"Why do you suppose the U.S. government has placed a post office here at this large store and mining operation?" the Baron continued.

E. Z. asked, "Aren't there post offices at other inns along the Natchez Trace?"

"Not like this one. This is a special office. Look at how large this inn is. Someone with your keen eye would recognize that it is far too large to be located here in The Wilderness," the Baron said, adding a flourish.

"I did think it was large," the captain admitted.

"But so was the one at Gordon's Ferry," E. Z. said.

"Another government secret," the Baron whispered. "But let us not digress. You can ask anyone how the Chickasaw boundary has moved south every few years. Settlers have been allowed to buy land in the areas that are opened up north of the boundary each time it moves south."

The captain added, "Now it is at the Tennessee Line at Grinder's."

The Baron shook his head. "That is what most people think. But it is not so. Only a few people know that as of three years ago, the true boundary by treaty is south of here, just north of the Tennessee River. And thus, this whole region is waiting to burst with settlement," the Baron said. He leaned over again to whisper. "That is why this mining operation and large inn are here. They are preparing for the major metropolis that is just a year or two away. Then it can be announced that settlers can move here, and they will arrive in droves to bid up land prices."

"I can see that now," the captain conceded, looking around. "And there is land available here?"

"Not here at this spot," the Baron said. "This land has already been claimed by people in Washington City and Nashville who know about the treaty. But there is still plenty of land just over a day's ride south. Enterprising settlers, who have been entrusted with the news, have already begun clearing the land. They are building cabins and fencing land as part of their claim."

"Who is selling the land? The government?" E. Z. asked.

"Indirectly. They have created land companies and appointed agents to issue deeds," the Baron said as he picked remnants of his dinner from his teeth. "I am agent for the Tennessee Land Company. That is why I said how fortuitous it was that you approached my table. I was just returning to Washington City with some deeds for land that has not sold yet. But... I could be persuaded to remain a day or two if any of your party would have an interest."

The captain was excited. "Young Ezekiel, I had begun to lose my optimism, and this just proves that persistence pays off. I will talk with our party, but I am sure that some will be interested. I am."

The Baron moved his chair back from the table and rested his hands on his large belly. "In that case, I shall change my travel plans and remain here another day or two. If you would like to examine the land, I shall meet you at your camp at breakfast time tomorrow and we shall travel together. If you have a wagon, I am certain that you have horses."

"Yes. A packhorse," the captain said. "You are welcome to travel with us."

The captain and E. Z. stood along with the Baron and shook hands. As they left the inn, the captain barely could contain his excitement.

E. Z. asked, "Why does a baron not have a horse?"

The captain answered, "Who knows what mission he is on? I am sure a man in his position has a whole stable of horses. Now that I think about it, it makes sense why the government built this new military road."

E. Z. added, "At least we won't have to travel much farther without knowing where we are going."

The captain reflected, "I will admit that after living through the Revolution and those difficult years in our new republic, I have had more excitement in my life than one man is entitled to experience. I do look forward to enjoying some peace on my own farm."

E. Z. said, "I'm sure that Ma would feel better too if we settled closer to the towns in Tennessee. At some point, the new towns will hire sheriffs to drive out the bandits."

As E. Z. and Captain Stark returned to camp to tell the party their good news, they found the group upset. Mr. Burton had not appeared. Worse, his disappearance meant that Esther, their packhorse, was missing. And along with her, the money that Sarah had hoped to recoup when Esther was sold to help buy their new farm.

Without money to buy land, E. Z.'s family would be homeless even if they survived the journey. Was Mr. Burton one of the ways The Devil's Backbone was fighting E. Z.?

CHAPTER FIFTEEN

Chickasaw Friends

Mr. Stewart had said little on the trip, but it was clear that he was upset. "I kept my eye on Mr. Burton, the best I could. I suspect that he had planned to take off with the horse at our first campsite. He almost did back at Swan Creek, but he changed his mind when Ezekiel went off into the woods."

"Why didn't you tell us?" Captain Stark asked.

"I had no proof," Mr. Stewart said, glancing at Sarah, "Everyone liked him. I kept trying to catch him, but he is wily. He caught on to me."

"When will we find men we can trust?" Sarah asked, her face showing her disappointment. It seemed clear to everyone that Sarah was concerned about more than the loss of the horse.

The captain responded, "That is what Young Ezekiel and I came to tell you. We met a... Mr. Baron, who is an agent for the government. He is selling land here in Tennessee, not more than a day's ride south. He passed along some government information about the plans for this area. He says this is where the money is to be made. The Mississippi Territory won't be a good investment for years."

"It would reduce our travel considerably if we could buy land here," Mary said.

"Mr. Baron is willing to show us the land tomorrow. He will ride down with us," the captain added.

"Now that we have lost the money we used to buy that horse, maybe we can use the money we will save on travel to still afford to buy land, " Mary said as she patted Sarah on the hand.

"I won't rest well tonight, worrying about whether we can afford it," Sarah said.

Mary tried to console her. "We have had so much trouble already, maybe things are about to improve. We had better get busy setting up our camp."

Captain Stark turned to the boys. "I spotted some large fish in the Buffalo River here as we rode up. Why don't you boys take your hooks and go down there and see if you can catch us a mess. We'll celebrate with a little fish fry."

The boys welcomed the opportunity to show off their new fishing skills and provide supper. But the traveling party was so upset, E. Z. also welcomed the permission for the boys to go off on their own for a few hours and play.

As the boys approached the slow-moving river, sounds of water running over the shallow rocks grew louder. In the shade, the river looked cool and inviting on a hot day. There were also places where the river had washed out the rocks to make the water deeper.

E. Z. laid down the hooks and suggested that they walk upstream and find a good place to take a swim first. E. Z. and David had grown up near a river. Despite Isaiah's brag about swimming the ocean, E. Z. had figured out that like David, Isaiah could not swim. E. Z. offered to teach them, and it did not take long until the boys learned how to stay afloat.

After proving who could swim the fastest and then taking turns to see who could hold his breath longest underwater, the boys turned to fishing. The captain had been correct. In no time, they caught all they would be able to eat for their supper. Playing in the river took their minds off the hazards of their trip. For a few minutes they forgot where they were and what challenges still lay ahead.

E. Z. was ready to gather the fish to take them back to camp when a familiar bark interrupted the quiet. All the boys recognized it. They looked up and saw Major standing on the opposite riverbank. Major gave another two quick barks before jumping into the river and paddling his way across to the boys.

"Major!" E. Z. shouted. E. Z. handed the fish to Isaiah and ran over to the water to greet their four-legged friend.

As soon as Major reached the bank, rather than running up to the boys as he had the last time they saw him, the dog fell down at E. Z.'s feet and closed his eyes.

"Is he dead?" Isaiah asked.

E. Z. squatted down to rub Major's head. "No, he's still breathing." But Major had several cuts. He was bleeding. Something had attacked him. "Let's see if we can carry him back to camp."

E. Z. and David took E. Z.'s floppy hat, turned it upside down, and gently lifted Major to place him in the hat to carry him to camp. The dog made a whimpering sound whenever they moved him.

When Mary saw E. Z. and David carrying something out of the woods, she first thought they were carrying Isaiah and panicked. "Isaiah!" she yelled out as she ran out to meet them, but then Isaiah walked out of the woods carrying the fish. She hugged her son and the fish at the same time.

Sarah walked over to examine Major. "Poor dog. He has been cut pretty bad. Bring him over to the camp."

The boys made a bed for Major out of straw. Captain Stark said he had seen wounds like those in the war. He held leaves and straw to staunch the bleeding and tied a few rags around Major to hold them in place. "Dogs heal quick. He'll be fine," the captain assessed.

E. Z. asked the captain, "What about Mister Johnson? Major wouldn't leave him unless…." He did not want to think about it. But he wondered whether Mr. Johnson was lying somewhere along the road with the same kind of wounds without anyone to bandage them. "Should we go looking for him?"

Mr. Stewart shook his head. "If you ask me, I am beginning to think that driver just abandoned us. He already had our money. He's probably rounding up another party in Nashville right now."

"Mr. Johnson wouldn't do that!" E. Z. protested.

"We'll see," Mr. Stewart said as he walked off to build the campfire.

The captain sat beside E. Z. "He just doesn't trust anybody. If you had been through what he has, you might not either. Now, back to Mr. Johnson. I don't know where we would begin to look for him," the captain said as he took out his fiddle and began tuning it.

E. Z. suspected that the captain wanted to look for Mr. Johnson, but whoever had attacked Major was still out there. This party was the captain's responsibility now. If they split up into smaller search parties, they would all be more vulnerable. There was safety in numbers. They would have to stay together and trust that the rangers were searching for Mr. Johnson.

Hannah filled a tin cup with cold water and sat down by Major in case the dog was thirsty. She sang songs to him and rubbed his ears.

The women fried the fish in bacon grease they had saved from their last stop. It would not be the celebration Captain Stark had planned. They had convinced themselves that Mister Johnson was safe somewhere. Major's injuries were evidence that he was not.

Captain Stark watched the children sit silently with their heads lowered. He began to play his fiddle.

Mr. Stewart seemed to notice the children's mood too. He said, "Once we have settled on our land, we can make another search for Mr. Johnson if the rangers have not found him by then."

Two Chickasaw boys from the inn were drawn to the campsite by the aroma of food. They walked down to the camp, stood at the edge, and stared at the fish. They looked hungry. The last advice Mr. Johnson had given before he disappeared was to do nothing to provoke the Indians. Without Mr. Johnson, no one was sure what to do.

Sarah handed a bowl of fish to the Chickasaws, who smiled and finished off the bowl in a few minutes. The Chickasaw boys then seated themselves by the fire and listened to Captain Stark play his fiddle.

The oldest Chickasaw boy noticed Major and went to examine him. He said something in Chickasaw to the younger boy. The younger walked over and began stroking Major's head. The older boy took something from a pouch he carried and placed it inside each of the bandages. E. Z. assumed that it was Indian medicine.

E. Z. walked over and sat by the boys. Talking slowly, he said, "My...name...is...Ezekiel. But...my...friends...call... me... 'E. Z.'" He pointed to his chest as he said his name.

The oldest boy repeated, "Easy."

"Yes," E. Z. said, impressed at how the boy repeated his name.

The Chickasaw boy pointed to his own chest, "Samuel," and then to his brother's, "Charles."

E. Z. laughed. "Those don't sound like Indian names."

Samuel laughed and said, "'Easy' not a white man name." Then, everybody laughed.

"My brother gave me that name," E. Z. said.

"How you win it?" Samuel said. His English was not clear, but he had grown up in so much contact with settlers, that they could understand him. He added, "Boys get new names when they become warriors. How many warriors you kill, E. Z.?"

E. Z. studied on that question. "I got the name for being a good brother."

David and Isaiah had hung back, a little afraid of the Indians. But once they saw that E. Z. showed no fear, they joined E. Z. and introduced themselves.

Charles spotted Isaiah's knife. His eyes widened. "Death knife."

"What?" David asked.

"Death knife," Charles repeated.

Samuel shouted to his brother in Chickasaw. He did not interpret.

"What's a 'death knife?'" Isaiah asked.

"Forget he said it," Samuel said.

Both Chickasaw boys turned to leave. Samuel hesitated, then returned.

He pointed to himself and then to E. Z. and said, "We friends, brothers."

E. Z. understood "friends," but "brothers?" How could they be brothers like E. Z. and David? Even though the boys were from different cultures, Samuel was suggesting a partnership. In his culture, he proposed that they would be loyal to each other and protect each other the same way E. Z. protected David.

To signify the agreement, Charles handed E. Z. a present of a small leather wristlet or bracelet with beads. E. Z. took the wristlet, "Thank you," he said as he put it on his wrist. "I am sorry that I have nothing to give you."

Samuel looked disappointed and turned to leave.

"Wait," E. Z. said. He reached into his hunting bag and pulled out two pieces of candy and handed them to Charles and Samuel. "It's sweet. It's good." E. Z. motioned to his mouth.

Samuel handed a piece of candy to Charles. Both boys put the candy in their mouths and smiled as they began to walk away. E. Z. was embarrassed that the presents he gave would disappear in minutes, but he was unprepared to make a gift.

E. Z. examined the beads on the wristlet. "Friends, brothers" was not what he was expecting from the Indians he had been warned to avoid.

Isaiah took his knife out of the sheath and began talking to it, "'Death knife,' I don't know where you have been, but you have a reputation in these parts."

Isaiah quickly hid the knife when he saw a man dressed in leather from head to foot, walking into camp from the woods. The woodsman even wore moccasins like Indians. The stranger asked if the party could share some food. Sarah handed him the last remnants of leftover fish on a tin plate. The man said that he was a trapper. He hunted in the Indian nations and bartered the animal hides to stores in Nashville.

Captain Stark tried to gain information from the trapper about what lay ahead for them in the area. The trapper knew nothing of the settlement the Baron was promoting. He had spent most of his time deep in the Indian nations.

But he was a quirky old man, and he made it clear that he avoided people as much as possible. He said that only hunger and good food would bring him out of hiding. "Kinda like the animals I trap."

The trapper said that he had seemed drawn to this group for some reason, and after he finished eating, he walked over to the fire to sit by the boys.

"Any of you seen a man wearin' an orange cloth coat?" the man asked.

The boys thought of the bandit's coat. E. Z. took the lead in replying, "We heard that a man wearing a bright cloth coat was killed on the road north of here. Why are you looking for him?"

The trapper did not seem surprised that the man was dead. "We had some unfinished business. Sounds like it will stay unfinished."

E. Z. said, "You can ask the rangers about him at Gordon's Ferry."

"Rangers!" the man spat as he said it. "Rangers don't care much for my kind. They'll run me out of the Indian country if they see me."

"Are you a bandit?" David asked.

"David!" E. Z. chided and rapped David on the head.

The old man laughed. "To them rangers I might as well be. They say anybody who buys somethin' from the Indians fair and square without goin' through their government agent first is the same as a robber. Have you ever heard of such in a free country?"

E. Z. thought of the map. "Did the man you are looking for have something that belonged to the Indians?" E. Z. asked.

"No. I can rightly say that he had nothin' that belonged to the Indians," the trapper said.

When Captain Stark walked over to the fire, the trapper changed the subject and said, "I am surprised that you camped at this spot. What drew you here?"

"We just happened to stop at the inn," E. Z. replied.

"But this ain't at the inn. Don't you know that this place was a center of the dead for tribes in the old days?"

The man pointed towards a spot on the riverbank and lowered his voice. "Those in charge of the dead would float bodies down the river to that spot. Then they would walk them up ramps in the banks and take them to funeral pyres. The pyres were almost at the spot where you built your fire. This is where they burned the bodies."

Isaiah joked, "I am glad we ate first. I wouldn't want to think about burning bodies on the fire where our food was."

As if on cue, an eagle soared overhead and let out a screech. Isaiah instinctively ducked.

The trapper looked up and smiled. He told the boys that if they listened carefully that night, they still could hear the boats bringing the dead to that spot. "Keep your fire burnin' for 'em and see what happens." The man grinned and walked away.

David watched the man disappear back into the woods and said, "Let's put the fire out now so that we don't confuse them."

"He is just having some fun by telling you stories," Captain Stark said. "Pay him no attention."

As the boys walked around the spot, they thought they saw the ramps the trapper had talked about. David pointed to large stones that seemed out of place. Maybe the trapper had been telling the truth.

David must have stayed awake most of the night listening to sounds on the river. He constantly woke E. Z. when he thought that the rippling of the water was the sound of the boats bringing the dead to the ramp. He said that he dreamed that he saw spirits of the Indian bodies that had been brought there dancing around the campfire.

E. Z. did not worry about the stranger's stories or the Chickasaws. He had his Chickasaw wristlet and new

Chickasaw friends. The area did not seem as foreign as it had.

Overnight, the Chickasaw medicine worked. Major rose first the next morning. He limped over to the boys, nuzzled them on their ears with his cold nose, and gave a quick bark to wake them.

The Baron invited himself to camp breakfast. He took two large helpings of biscuits and bacon, as he looked around to see if there was more. E. Z. noticed that Sarah put her plate back, because there would not have been enough for the children to eat if she took her part.

After breakfast, the Baron unfolded two maps of the area. One was drawn by the army. The Baron pointed to their current location. Then he pointed to the area where he said land was available just north of the Tennessee River. He showed the same area on his map of the parcels of land. Several families had already begun clearing farms and building cabins.

Captain Stark looked at the Baron's map as if it had been the copy of the map E. Z. carried in his boot that he hoped would lead to treasure.

The Baron said, "I had planned to show you the land. I regret that I have been called back to Nashville to meet with new investors who are arriving to discuss building the new towns."

Captain Stark looked disappointed. "We had planned to buy that land today and begin clearing it."

"Well..." the Baron said, placing his hand on his head as he pretended to figure out a solution. "Now, when the government gave you a deed to land for your service with General Washington, I take it you had not seen the land?"

"No. I had to rely on people in the area to select it. And I have to say that they picked out a valuable piece," the captain said.

"That's because people most familiar with the land know the best tracts. In honor of your service, I have selected some of the best remaining parcels for you." The Baron took deeds out of his pocket, and then he marked where the land was located on the map. "See how close these are to the river? This is rich bottom land. Many settlers are beginning to grow cotton. This far south, cotton will grow practically year-round! And you will have but a short distance to transport it to the river to float it to Natchez to market."

"Well, that does look promising," the captain said as he looked to the others.

Mr. Stewart said, "I don't know that we should buy land that we have not already seen."

Sarah added, "Please don't be offended. We have just met you."

"That is quite alright," the Baron said. "I anticipated your concern, and here is the solution I propose. If you will pay me but one-half the price for the land, I shall trust you to pay the remainder. I shall return within the month to collect the rest. If, during that time, you have decided that the land is not suitable, you may return the deeds and I shall refund your payments."

Captain Stark looked at the others. "That certainly seems fair."

Mr. Stewart frowned. "What is the price of the land?"

The Baron laid deeds on the map and marked their locations. "I have taken the liberty of writing the prices on each deed. You will see that the prices are very reasonable, and the land will be a good investment."

Sarah and the men glanced over at the deeds. Sarah sighed in relief when she saw the price on the smallest parcel. The Baron watched her eyes. "I priced that parcel just for you," he said with a wink.

The group asked if they could discuss the land in private. The Baron said that he understood. He looked for a shady spot under a tree and asked David to fetch him a chair and to bring him a cup of water. E. Z. tagged along with the adults to see what his mother would decide.

The captain led the discussion. They had lost much of their money to buy land when Mr. Burton disappeared with Esther. There was no assurance that even if they found other land in the Mississippi Territory they could afford it. Buying this land seemed to be the only way they could be certain they would have funds to buy farms. They did not know the Baron, but he looked reliable and he would be returning the next week if there were any problems.

Mr. Stewart acted as if he wanted to say more, but it seemed clear that he did not want to disappoint Sarah. It was settled. They would take the land.

Sarah said that she felt as if a load had been lifted from her shoulders as she could see that the trip had not been a mistake. She showed the deed and the map to E. Z. and David, encouraging them they should arrive at their new home later that day.

The Baron looked pleased. He completed the deeds on behalf of the Tennessee Land Company by signing his name with a large flourish. As the Baron folded the party's money into a leather pouch, he added, "Now, rest assured that you can return your deeds next week if there is anything about this land that does not suit you."

E. Z. suspected that the Baron would probably use some of the money to buy a horse for his trip to Nashville.

With the deeds in hand, the party boarded the wagon and headed south on the Natchez Trace to their new home. E. Z. hoped the biggest challenges of the road were behind him. He had survived.

Later, he would conclude that he was being tricked into letting down his guard.

CHAPTER SIXTEEN

Jack, the Bully

The promise of a new home and the hope of a new start lifted the spirits of the party. Captain Stark began singing. The boys did not know the song, but they joined in as best they could—loud and off-tune.

Major lay at their feet. The dog still whimpered from pain, but his eyes were bright. Once, Major barked at a squirrel running across a limb directly over their wagon.

E. Z. had not forgotten about Mr. Johnson, Jack, the bandit, Mr. Burton, or the map. A few times, he stood to look behind them to see if anyone was following.

Now that the travelers were closer to finding their new land, their more immediate concern was how to create some shelter once they arrived. The Perkins boys were not strong enough yet to build a cabin. The lower Mississippi area where they had planned to go would be filled with

179

settlers who could help. They did not know whether this new area would be the same.

Captain Stark faced the same problem. He was too old to build a cabin by himself, and Mr. Stewart did not appear to be the cabin-building type.

The captain was always optimistic. "Cabins take time. I have heard of families living in large, hollow trees the first winter until they have time to build. In summer, you could make a brush arbor or grass hut. We can learn from the Indians. They have lived in these parts for years and only recently have they begun building cabins. They survive. We can too."

About noon, the captain pulled the wagon to a stop by a shady spring. "As Mr. Johnson would say, fill your canteens and take care of anything else," the captain said, helping the ladies out of the wagon. "I'll feed the oxen and see after Major."

The boys ran down to a creek to see if there were any fish they could catch to add to their dinner. They found nothing larger than a minnow.

Isaiah picked one up, and joked, "This minnow and a hundred more will add up to one fish for the one man of your family. I hope the fishing is better at our new home."

"I hope a lot of things are better at our new home," David added.

"Things can't get much worse than the past few days. We have gone through the fire as Mr. Johnson said we would. So far, we are surviving," E. Z. said.

A large fish jumped up in the creek. E. Z. pulled off his boots and rolled up his pants legs. He handed the boots and hunting bag to David. "Here, hold on to these. I am going to see if I can catch that fish with my hands. We don't have time to get the hooks."

E. Z. followed the fish through a channel to the side of the creek. The fish must have caught the sight of something large coming toward it. It began swimming faster to follow the deeper part of the stream.

E. Z. chased the fish around a bend where the water deepened. He bent down, putting his hand near one side of the fish, but then his feet slipped on the rock beneath the water. A slimy moss had formed on the limestone on the creek bed, making it almost as slick as glass. The fish barely escaped his reach.

E. Z. chased the fish around a second bend in the creek, and then a third, each time keeping a glimpse of the back of the fish. For a moment, E. Z. had second thoughts about catching it. He knew how the fish felt. He could see himself as that fish on the Natchez Trace as someone was trying to trap him.

"Did you catch him? We're getting hungry," Isaiah yelled from upstream, nearly out of hearing.

"I've almost got him. He's smart, though. He knows I'm after him," E. Z. said.

E. Z. had the idea to run ahead of the fish and trap it, using some tree limbs he saw near the stream. He ran down two more bends in the creek to a spot where the shallow water might slow the fish. He rolled his pants legs up higher.

As E. Z. neared the shallow area, the surface of the rocks became slicker. E. Z.'s feet ran in a different direction than his head, and he fell headlong into the water. His head plunged beneath the surface, barely missing sharp rocks.

E. Z. sat up and spat out a mouthful of water. He thought he might have swallowed a minnow. As he coughed and rubbed the water from his hair and his eyes, an extended hand appeared in front of him. Then he smelled pigs. It was Jack!

"My good ole friend, E. Z. Are you catchin' fish or are they catchin' you?" Jack laughed. Then his smile turned to the villain smile. "Either way, I caught you."

E. Z. made a quick swipe toward Jack's feet, hoping that Jack would not realize how slick the rocks were in the water and that it would throw him off-balance. But Jack only stepped back.

"I don't wanna fight you, E. Z." Jack pulled out his knife. "And I don't rightly believe that you wanna fight me neither." Jack pointed back upstream. "I seen yore brother and yore other friend. But he's not carryin' my knife."

E. Z.'s heart pounded. He wondered whether Jack had hurt David or Isaiah. If he had, E. Z. determined to tackle him, knife, or no knife.

Jack could see what E. Z. was thinking. "Don't worry. Yore brother and other friend are a little too close to your party fer me to take chances. But yo're not. I thought this might be a good time to catch you alone to finish our business before you left my road."

"We don't have any business. Do you have nothing better to do than to follow me just to make my life miserable?" E. Z. said as he pushed himself up on the rocks to stand up.

Jack laughed and spat. "Aw, E. Z. As much as I enjoy our little git-togethers, yo're not the reason I'm followin' you and you know it. As soon as you give me that knife, that huntin' bag, and that map, you won't ever see me again. I can promise you that." Jack's tone left the impression that E. Z. would never see anything again once Jack had what he wanted.

E. Z. held out his hands. "Look, do you see any knife, bag, or map?"

"I'm not stupid. I know they're back at yore wagon." Jack held out his own knife. "Now, how about you call yore little brother here while you go look fer 'em. I'll mind him fer you. I'll take *real good* care of him."

E. Z. needed time to think of a plan. He made a show of wiping off water to take longer to answer Jack. He could shout for the others, but there was no one who could provide any help. He still did not know whether Mr. Stewart was dependable.

"What makes you think that what I have is a map?" E. Z. said.

"The ghost told me what it was," Jack said.

E. Z. acted as if he were turning to leave. "Alright, maybe I can go look to see if I can find one. Tell me first what it is a map of. The curiosity will drive me crazy if I never find out."

Jack said, "You don't wanna know. Even if you followed it, you wouldn't live to get out."

"So, what good will it do you?" E. Z. asked.

"I said that *you* wouldn't live to get out. I got friends. Yo're not one of those friends that can help in those kinds of places. Now, you goin' to git it or not?"

E. Z. stalled. "Do you know what happened to our driver?"

Jack fidgeted, scratched himself under his arms, and looked down. "I know everything that happens on this road." He looked like he wanted to say more but only added, "That dog is yore's now."

E. Z.'s stomach cramped as if Jack had punched him. He had held out hope that Mr. Johnson was still alive and ready to return to the wagon.

Jack moved his knife closer. "Alright, then. Enough talk. I've got a long ways to go once you give me what y'ore carryin."

E. Z. still had to figure out an escape for all three boys. He turned to stand squarely facing Jack and said, "I changed my mind. Fight me for it!"

This time, Jack's head drew back as if he had been hit. "What'd you say?"

"I said, 'Fight me for it.'" E. Z. stared right at Jack to show that he meant it. "I'll prove to you I can help you find whatever is on that map."

Jack was clearly taken aback, but it did not take him long to recover. He smirked. "E. Z., has anybody told you that we don't fight fair here?" Jack brandished his knife and walked toward E. Z. "Let's say I give you a little lesson to show you what I mean."

Jack's knife pinged and suddenly flew out of his hand as a shot rang out from the direction where E. Z. had left David and Isaiah. To E. Z., seeing the look of shock on Jack's face was worth the bluff he had played.

Jack shook his hand in pain. He took a quick glance toward the source of the shot and then ran behind a bush.

"We'll meet again, E. Z. I never give up." With that promise, Jack ran off.

But who had shot? E. Z. had no way of knowing whether it was from a friend or enemy, but it came from where he had left David and Isaiah. E. Z. ran back upstream as fast as he could on the slick rocks. When E. Z. arrived, he was shocked to see Mr. Burton sitting and talking with David and Isaiah.

Mr. Burton looked up. "That makes twice now, Ezekiel. You did not take my advice."

"Where have you been? I thought you took off," E. Z. said.

"I would not leave your mother—and you boys—out here on your own if it hadn't been necessary. We'll talk about it later." Giving E. Z. a quick glance from side to side, Mr. Burton said, "It looks like you escaped without injury. I don't see any blood."

"Thank you... again," E. Z. said. "I didn't thank you before."

Mr. Burton smiled. "I told you when we met that we would become good friends. I didn't think I would have to prove it so soon."

David and Isaiah wanted to hear more about Jack as E. Z. stooped to put on his boots. E. Z. first glanced inside to make sure that the map was still there.

As they walked back to where the others were preparing for dinner, E. Z. told Mr. Burton about Jack and about the bandit. He stopped short of mentioning the map or that he had suspected Mr. Burton of following them and attempting to take the map. E. Z. was grateful that Mr. Burton came along when he did.

The party rushed out to greet E. Z. as they had the first time he had disappeared. When E. Z. saw the wagon, Major, and his mother, he dropped his head. As much as he wanted to talk, the words would not come out. After a few minutes, he haltingly told the party about Jack and that Jack had given him the impression that Mr. Johnson was dead.

Mr. Burton acted almost relieved that the story about Jack and Mr. Johnson took attention away from him. And Esther. He had not stolen her after all. Sarah showed appreciation that their investment in the horse was safe for the moment. E. Z. grew frustrated at the thought that his mother was almost thanking Mr. Burton for not stealing their property.

The mothers finished unpacking the food. E. Z. told them about the fish that got away that would have added to their meal.

As the party sat by the evening campfire, all attention focused on Mr. Burton. Everyone noticed that he chose to sit close to Sarah.

Then Mr. Burton began his explanation, "I got news that there were men out on the Natchez Trace following us. Ezekiel, one was the boy you call 'Jack,' but there are more. I rode out to try to trick them into heading off down a different path. At least with Jack, I was able to provide a little help."

Sarah put her hand on Mr. Burton's hand and thanked him for saving E. Z. twice. Mr. Burton's eyes lit up. Hannah looked across the fire at E. Z. and smiled as if to brag that her secret had been correct. E. Z. looked back with a stare meant to say that his secret about a bandit wanting to follow them had been correct too.

E. Z. remembered the Franklin storeowner's advice. "Bandits come in all forms." Was Mr. Burton a bandit who was trying to steal his mother? Only time would tell.

Mr. Burton showed disappointment to hear that travel plans had changed. He had been headed for the Mississippi Territory. Now, the party planned to stop north of the Tennessee River.

Mr. Burton's face flashed with anger when he heard that Sarah and the others had paid the Baron for land. He waited a few minutes as he searched for words. "There is no good way to give you bad news. The 'Baron' is a swindler. He is not a baron, and he has no land. He doesn't even own a horse."

E. Z. glanced at Captain Stark whose gaze dropped to the ground. The Captain's face turned pale. There was silence as the party tried to think through what it meant that they had given away most of the money they had saved for land. Now, they were trapped.

"I can try to track him down," Mr. Burton said. "But based on his history, he has already gambled your money away. He won't have any more until he swindles the next party."

Sarah began to cry. Mary's sobs were louder. When the captain saw the women's pain, tears rolled down his face. He said it had all been his fault. He apologized.

Sarah tried to comfort him, "We're all very much 'babes in the woods.' This is an unknown world for us. Captain, you are no more to blame than any of the rest of us." It had seemed too good to be true, and it was.

"So, there is no settlement just ahead?" Mr. Stewart asked.

Mr. Burton said, "Oh, there is a settlement. That much is true. People are clearing the land and building cabins. They hope that they will have the first chance to buy the land when the government puts it up for sale. Who knows when that will be? It is still considered Chickasaw land."

Again, there was a long pause as everyone thought through the options. Sarah broke the silence, "What choice do we have? We are out of money and our supplies are limited. We have nowhere else to go." She said that she had to think about her sons.

Captain Stark said, "We are less than a day away. What could it hurt to march on and have a look?"

Sarah turned to Mr. Burton. "Will you be leaving us to go on down to the Mississippi Territory?"

E. Z. watched Mr. Burton closely to see whether his response would be genuine.

Mr. Burton said, "I should, but first I will make sure that you are all settled in. You may need some help building cabins."

That much was good news to the boys. Living in a hollow tree for a while sounded like adventure, but their mothers would want real houses. On winter evenings, they would all want fireplaces to sit near instead of a small fire that filled a tree with smoke.

As soon as they had eaten, with the uncertainty of what they would find at the settlement, no one wasted time packing up to move on. The wagon traveled up and down the rolling hills that gradually flattened the farther south they traveled. The party had planned to arrive at the new settlement before dark. But the day's events had delayed them. Near dusk, Captain Stark stopped to make camp near a spring.

As they did most evenings after supper, the party sat around the campfire to talk about the day's events and to plan for the next day. The glow and crackling of campfire was familiar and comforting. It encouraged strangers to talk and created a sense of community for people who might be destined to become neighbors the rest of their lives.

No one mentioned Mr. Stewart's earlier accusations about Mr. Burton. Mr. Stewart sat away from the fire with his back resting on a tree and watched Mr. Burton from a distance. E. Z. watched Mr. Burton closer from across the fire.

Captain Stark said that he still felt responsible for encouraging everyone to trust the Baron. He brought out his fiddle, but he only placed it in his lap and avoided looking at anyone.

E. Z. and Isaiah sat by the captain and requested a tune. The captain was reluctant, but then he began to play, and the music took his mind off their predicament. To lighten the mood, E. Z. asked if he should dispense more candy. The captain agreed.

The party could not rest completely. There was one more night on the Devil's Backbone. One more night to worry about Jack and the bandit. If a gang was still following them, this should be its last opportunity to attack the party on the road.

The boys made a straw bed for Major near their pallet. Hanna took Esther some extra corn. Sarah carried a piece of cornbread that she had saved at supper along with a cup of hot coffee to Mr. Burton. He had agreed to take the first watch as the others slept. The two sat by the campfire alone and talked late into the night.

E. Z. wrestled with the idea of telling Mr. Burton about the map to see if he recognized the area where it led. If Mr. Burton would be going with them, there would be time enough for that. Mr. Burton had at least proved himself in saving E. Z. from Jack. Once Sarah was asleep, there seemed to be no point in E. Z. trying to avoid sleep to keep an eye on him.

If E. Z. had stayed awake, he could have looked just outside their camp and seen a familiar glistening reflecting the campfire in the woods. Mr. Burton saw it. He said nothing. He raised his pistol in its direction, and it disappeared. Like Mr. Burton, Jack also must have decided that there was still time enough for his plans.

CHAPTER SEVENTEEN

Sinking Creek Militia

The next morning, E. Z. was relieved finally to leave The Devil's Backbone. After the wagon had left the Natchez Trace and traveled only a few miles over rough land that had no road, Captain Stark said this route must be the Devil's sister.

Oxen were not the brightest animals. On the Natchez Trace, they could follow the well-worn road. It took Captain Stark's full attention to keep them pressing ahead in the direction he wanted across open fields and along dry creek beds. E. Z. tried helping by singing to Jim and Ole Henry.

Mr. Burton suggested that he ride Esther in front of the oxen and maybe the oxen would follow his lead. E. Z. wondered whether Mr. Burton was making an excuse to disappear again.

The wagon jostled everyone inside as it hit rocks and stumps. The wheel that Mr. Johnson had repaired held.

Even though the Baron was a swindler, his map proved correct according to Mr. Burton. He said that the best swindlers used the truth as far as it would take them to win their victim's trust.

As the wagon began to descend from the ridge to the area where the Baron's map led, two or three farms appeared on the horizon. Cabins had been built near the center. Captain Stark stopped the wagon so that everyone could get a look. He smiled when he saw that he had led them to a settlement after all. Maybe it would all still work out.

The captain drove the oxen faster in anticipation of finding their new home. He stopped at the first cabin. A couple of farmers had seen the wagon descending the ridge and walked up to find out whether the travelers were friends or enemies.

The older farmer introduced himself as Henry Smith. The boy with him was his son Jessie. Jessie was a year younger than E. Z., but he was just as tall, and heavier, "big boned" is how he described it. Jessie chewed nervously on a willow tree limb, obviously sizing up the boys as competition in games they played on the farm.

Mr. Smith took off his hat and used it to fan his face. He said they had been girdling trees all morning. The trees were too wide to chop down. The farmers had to put girdles made of iron around them to cut off the flow of sap to kill them. Within a few years, windstorms would blow down the trees and then they could burn them. That was how settlers cleared the land for farms.

E. Z. realized that the Perkins brothers had hard work ahead of them. It would be years, if ever, before E. Z. became the farmer he had seen in Nashville admiring his crops from an easy chair on his porch.

Mr. Smith's wife invited the party to join her family for the midday dinner. She told them where to find water to wash their hands and faces.

After they ate, Jessie encouraged the boys to go with him to see his favorite fishing spot. They could catch fish for supper. E. Z. wanted Major to join them, but Captain Stark said that Major needed to rest for a few days. The captain would see after him.

On the way to the creek, Jessie led the boys by another farm occupied by the Hart family. The Harts had twin sons, Elijah and Nathaniel, dark-haired and dark-tanned twelve-year-olds. If it were possible to bottle up the energy from the storm on the Cumberland River and split it between two boys, that would describe the twins. They were in constant motion. The only way to tell them apart was that Elijah had a scar on his right cheek that he got from a fight with a rooster when he was three.

Introductions were made all around. Isaiah proudly showed his knife. E. Z. displayed his hunting bag. The farm boys were duly impressed. They showed the new boys large Indian arrows they had found near their cabins.

"Are there Indians close by?" David asked.

Jessie said, "We see Chickasaw and Cherokee all the time. Sometimes a few Choctaw. You will learn to tell the difference. They come up to trade at the store."

"There is a store here?" E. Z. asked.

Jessie pointed. "Over there. An old man came down from Nashville and opened one a few months ago. We take pelts to him and trade for what we need."

The farm boys welcomed their new friends and new competitors to sharpen their own skills. It did not take E. Z. long to figure out which boy thought of himself as best at each. Nathaniel suggested that they race to the creek. He hoped to prove that he was still the fastest boy on Sinking Creek. As soon as they came to the creek, Jessie challenged everyone to wrestle. None of the other boys would be able to take him down in a fight.

Elijah was good at neither. He challenged the boys to a shooting contest. But first they would have to bring in enough pelts to trade for powder and bullets. Nathaniel joked that his twin brother was practicing to be a bandit on The Devil's Backbone.

That joke opened the door for E. Z., David, and Isaiah to tell their adventures on the Natchez Trace. Storytelling continued through the afternoon through swimming and fishing.

The fishing hole looked promising. E. Z. could see large bass and catfish swimming in the water. It must have been his imagination, but once he thought he saw the fish he had tried to trap back on the Natchez Trace.

The boys lugged a large catch of fish back home for supper. Instead of joining the adult's meal, they carried their food down to the creek, and made their own campfire to continue storytelling.

Nathaniel and Elijah practiced throwing a tomahawk at a tree as they carried on the conversation. The twins seemed to be lost in their own world until it was time for them to speak. Then, it became obvious that all their activity helped them listen. The twins missed no detail.

E. Z. learned that even though the farms were some distance from the Natchez Trace, bandits sometimes rode off the road and through their area. And there were always stories that Creek Indians had gone to war against the settlers and that they were preparing to attack.

E. Z. said, "We met Chickasaws at McLish's inn. They weren't what we expected. I think we became friends."

"The Chickasaws are friends. But there are Creek and Shawnee that do not want us here. They are absolutely as dangerous as you heard," Elijah said.

"How can you tell if their warriors are in the area?" David asked.

"You can't. Sometimes the Chickasaws warn us to be on watch."

Bandits and Indians even on Sinking Creek! E. Z. was not free of the Natchez Trace challenge yet. But new farm friends meant safety in numbers. In the back of his mind, E. Z. also took some comfort in the fact that Mr. Burton was still around. Mr. Burton could provide some help toward E. Z.'s obligation to protect his mother and David.

The travelers had no shelter of their own yet. Some of the families invited the adults to stay with them in their cabins until they had time to build. Nathaniel and Elijah decided that all the boys could sleep in their barn loft. It made no difference to the boys whether the barn was comfortable so long as they were spending time with their new friends.

There were so many stories to share that none of the boys could go to sleep until late. E. Z. saved his best stories about the Natchez Trace until bedtime. He asked whether any of the boys had ever heard of Jack, but of course no one knew him by that name. The farm boys did not act worried that a group of bandits had followed the party. It was apparently a common danger they had learned to live with.

Elijah suggested that they form their own militia. They could practice their shooting and prepare to defend themselves from whoever attacked their homes. He proposed that they should call themselves "The Sinking Creek Militia." When the area finally became part of the state, they could use their experience to be elected officers of their company.

The farm boys said they had seen Mr. Johnson a few times when they had made the two-day trip to McLish's Stand to trade and store up food for winter. "Honestly, we were afraid of him," Nathaniel said. "He snarled at anybody who wasn't riding with him."

"Most people in this area snarl at strangers," Jessie added. "There are so many people passing through that you never know who anyone is. If you snarl at people, they usually leave you alone and don't take advantage of you."

"It works for bobcats," Nathaniel added.

"You haven't snarled at us yet," Isaiah said with a grin.

"You don't look dangerous," Jessie said. Isaiah's smile disappeared with disappointment that no one was afraid of him.

Nathaniel asked, "Do you hunt?"

"Hunt what?" E. Z. asked.

The farm boys looked at each other and smiled. They were ready to make fun of the boys from the East, until E. Z. mentioned that his father had died when he was young. Jessie suggested that the boys go hunting the next morning.

"We don't have a gun," David said.

Nathaniel said, "You don't need one. Without a gun, you just have to be cleverer than whatever it is you are hunting."

"What will we hunt?" E. Z. asked.

"How about panther? That pelt will bring some money," Elijah said.

David looked at E. Z. with more than a little fright.

"You need a gun to hunt panther," Nathaniel said.

David nodded and agreed, "That's right, you do."

"How about deer?" Elijah offered. "We have some extra bows. We'll have some fresh venison for supper. A good thing about living here, boys, is that you just step out your back door and your supper comes walking by."

"Unless whatever walks by is bigger than you, then you're supper," Jessie said as he laughed.

It was settled. The boys would rise before sunrise and go out to hunt deer.

As the boys worked to calm the excitement of their stories to try to fall asleep, something large rattled the barn roof as it crawled across it.

"What was that?" Elijah asked, as he sat up.

"Remind me to tell you about the ghost that's following me," E. Z. said.

"Don't start telling ghost stories or we'll never go to sleep," Jessie said.

E. Z. agreed. And he stayed quiet even when he heard the barn door open and shut. He was not worried. He now had his own militia and there was safety in numbers.

CHAPTER EIGHTEEN

Torches

———

The next morning, David was the last boy to wake up. "Why are we going out while it is still dark? We can't even see the deer yet."

"We have to be there when the deer wake up and go out to forage," Elijah said. "We have to catch them when they don't expect us."

Jessie said, "I have an idea. Let's paint ourselves as Indian warriors and hunt like Indians. The deer are the enemy. Who can the deer be?"

Nathaniel joked, "If we're Indians, they can be the people who live on Sinking Creek." Nathaniel emphasized his point by jumping on his brother's back and wrestling him to the ground.

Elijah rolled his brother over and got the upper hand. "That's us. That's not funny. Pa won't think it funny either when he shoots one of us by mistake."

As the Hart brothers fought in the hay, Jessie rubbed bear grease on a wooden bow to make it bend easier. He showed E. Z. how to take three fingers to pull the bow back to shoot an arrow. "Of course, the bow is made to match the size of the man. You're about my size so this one ought to work."

E. Z. tried first pulling with his arms.

"You're doing it wrong," Elijah said as he squirmed out of a wrestling hold and brushed hay off his shirt. "You have to use your back to pull the bow back. That will give the arrow more power."

"Like this?" E. Z. showed his strength as the arrow flew fast but missed a board that the farm boys used for practice.

"It takes time, but you've got the idea. Just figure that the arrow goes up before it goes down. Aim a little high," Nathaniel said, before catching his brother off guard and throwing him in another wrestling hold.

E. Z. showed Isaiah and David what he had learned. He knew that it would take them longer to learn, and the Sinking Creek boys would not have the patience.

The farm boys led the way into the woods. They showed the new boys how to look for two small depressions in the dirt from deer hooves. It was too dry to see them anywhere except near the creek.

E. Z. followed Jessie's lead around the edge of the creek. They spotted pairs of tracks and followed them.

Then, the boys saw him—a tall deer buck with a small set of horns that showed his young age.

"He's yours, E. Z. Remember what we showed you," Jessie whispered as he fidgeted with his own bow in anticipation.

E. Z. pulled back and aimed slightly high before letting go. The arrow barely missed its target. Jessie shot immediately just ahead of the deer as it ran away and took it down.

If Jack were watching from somewhere in the woods, he could see how quickly E. Z. was learning to use a bow. Jack might be impressed that he would have to act faster to take the map.

The Sinking Creek boys walked over to the fallen deer and bowed their heads.

"What are you doing now?" E. Z. asked.

"We learned this from the Indians. They give thanks to the animals that give their lives to provide food," Elijah said.

Nathaniel corrected his brother. "We learned the bowing from a circuit preacher who thanked God for the animals."

The boys used their hatchets to cut two large sticks to form a bier to carry the deer back home. The adults welcomed the fresh venison. Everyone decided they would have a community supper and celebrate their new neighbors.

At breakfast, E. Z. noticed that the worry Sarah had shown since they arrived in Nashville began to disappear.

E. Z. heard her tell Mary, "I think this is a good place for my sons to learn to become men."

Sarah said that she wanted to waste no time checking to see whether the land in the Baron's deed was occupied. The deed was worthless, but Sarah had paid good money for it. She said that maybe she would be able to use that payment to argue that she should be given the first right to buy it.

Mr. Burton took the Baron's map and joined Sarah and the boys to find the land. Her mood lightened even more when she saw that the land was open as she had hoped. There was a small rise that would make a good place to build a cabin. A spring that would provide fresh water was only a few steps away. The boys could look over a valley and see for what they thought must be a mile. The soil in the valley would be best for growing crops.

Mr. Burton walked around with the boys to scout trees that could be cut to make logs for the cabin.

"We—or I mean, you—need to find chestnut to use for the walls and floor. It is a hard wood that will last a long time. Then you need a softer wood like poplar for doors, window shutters, hinges, and other things that take some shaping," he said.

The tract Sarah claimed had plenty of each. If the farm families pitched in to help, they should have a cabin up in time for winter.

As they returned to where the house would be built, E. Z. showed off his new knowledge by pointing out a couple deer tracks. Then, he spotted horse tracks. Mr. Burton saw them too but did not mention them.

"How soon can we begin?" Sarah asked.

"I'm ready," E. Z. said. "I like it here. Don't you, David?"

"As long as we don't have to hunt panther," he said, without looking up from his drawing of where the buildings would be built.

The Stewart family said that they had also found land that would be a good place to build their cabins. Captain Stark decided that he would build a small room for himself that he would tie on to the Stewart's cabin. The captain had even picked out a spot overlooking the valley where he said he wanted to be buried when the time came.

When the travelers returned to the settlement, supper was waiting. The leftover deer had been put into a pot for a stew feast for the families so that it would not spoil. The adults made a point to complement the boys for their contribution for supper, making them the heroes.

The Perkins and Stewarts told the others about the farms they planned to occupy. The Sinking Creek families assured the travelers they would be welcome to join the community. All would pitch in to help build the cabins for winter. Barns would have to wait until the following spring, but the travelers would have nothing to put into a barn until the following harvest year. It would take them some time anyway to clear any land to farm. Until then, they could live off hunting.

After supper, the boys returned to the barn, "Fort Sinking Creek" as they began calling it. They discussed assigning one of the boys to be a sentinel for the evening to keep watch outside. But no one wanted to miss the talk inside. Nathaniel tried standing, bow in hand, at attention at the edge of the loft. But he finally gave up and joined the rest for stories.

The farm boys could not wait to hear about E. Z.'s ghost. They had a few stories of their own to tell first, but they had to admit that most of theirs were made up.

E. Z. began his story at the point he met the bandit at the inn. Then told about walking into the church building to see the body. The Sinking Creek boys barely breathed as E. Z. talked about moving the man's hand and mentioned the body sitting up. E. Z. showed them the scratches on his hand from the claws. David shuddered.

"Jack says that the man's ghost is following me. He says he has seen him in the woods behind me," E. Z. said.

"Why would you trust anything Jack tells you?" Jessie asked.

"Mr. Burton says that he also saw someone at the cave. He shot at him," E. Z. said. "We keep finding painted metal pieces like the ones on the body's eyes at places where the ghost seems to be."

"What happened to the map?" Nathaniel asked.

E. Z. thought a moment. He trusted his new friends. He reached over for his boot and pulled the map out.

"Don't open it. It's cursed," David said. The farm boys laughed.

The boys had only a small lamp for light in the barn. They added a second wick to make it brighter.

"Snakes!" the Sinking Creek boys all said as E. Z. spread out the map.

"What do you think it means? Does it look like anyplace you have seen?" E. Z. asked.

Nathaniel studied it. "I think the snakes are either roads or rivers."

"Why?"

"They are leading to someplace. Out here, you only have three choices: a trail, a road, and a river. Whoever uses the map must be able to follow them to where that "X" is," Nathaniel said.

"What happened to the rest of the map?" Ezekiel asked.

"This is all the map showed," E. Z. said.

E. Z. asked David to pass him his other boot. He pulled out a second map. "The Captain handed me this one. It is the one the Baron gave our parents for this area. Maybe you can spot something on the map in this area that matches the snake map."

E. Z. put the two maps side by side. One was a copy of a map drawn by an army mapmaker. The second was David's copy. They were nothing alike.

Jessie held up David's map. "This map is awful. Who drew this?" Jessie asked.

David sat up and looked Jessie in the eyes. "Have you ever tried drawing a map in the dark with a dead man just waiting for you to finish so that he could chase you down and take it from you?" David might shy away from a panther hunt, but criticism of his drawings brought out the warrior in him.

Jessie said, "I'm glad to see you have some spirit after all. That will make our militia stronger."

"Wait! Do you see it?" Nathaniel pointed to the two maps. "Look at that snake's head and tail! Now, look at the army map. See, it's there!"

"I don't see a snake on the army map," Nathaniel said.

"No. The river. The river is shaped the same as the snake. And the snake is shaped the same as the river," Nathaniel continued. After he pointed out the similarity, the boys could see it.

E. Z. saw it as if it popped up off the map. "But what is the snake that stands up straight? No, wait. I see it! I see it!"

The barn door slammed below. E. Z. did not wait for the others to follow. He jumped from the loft to see who had been hiding inside. Jessie followed right behind him. David would not stay behind without E. Z. He crawled down the loft ladder. The others followed.

E. Z. looked outside and saw no one.

David spotted two painted metal pieces on the ground. "It's the ghost. See, I told you the map is cursed," David said.

"I think it's Jack. He wants us to think it is the ghost," E. Z. said. "Now Jack knows where one point is on the map. At least I didn't tell him the other two."

The boys returned to the loft. They speculated on what might be where the "X" was located. E. Z. promised to share whatever it was with the "militia" if they helped him find it. Everyone shook on it.

E. Z. continued talking about the ghost. There was always the possibility that the bandit had not been dead as people in Franklin had speculated. In that case, the bandit and his bandit friends knew that E. Z. had a copy of his map. "The storeowner in Franklin told me that sometimes a person everyone assumes to be dead is really just sick or stunned. They'll get up in the middle of their funeral."

"I'd like to see that," Isaiah said.

"How do they know if the person is dead?" Nathaniel asked.

E. Z. said, "They put a looking glass up to the body's nose. If it is breathing, the looking glass will fog over from its breath."

Jessie asked, "Did you test the body before you moved its hand?"

"No. I didn't know there was any chance he was still alive," E. Z. said.

"He wasn't alive," David said. "He's a ghost."

Both wicks on the lamp burned dim. The farm boys turned to stories of wild animals in the area. Sometimes they added extra heads to make the stories more interesting.

E. Z. told the boys of seeing a glimpse of the hairy creature and Mr. Johnson's description of the one Major feared.

By the time storytelling had finished, David had moved to the center of the group. Whatever might enter the barn that night would have to get through two boys before it reached him.

They had all fallen asleep when gunshots rang out. Then shouts. Lots of them. Shots could be heard coming from three different places.

E. Z.'s first suspicions were that Jack's bandit gang had come for the map. The boys were defenseless several hundred yards from the nearest cabin. The other boys heard the sounds at the same time and opened their eyes.

Next came a loud roar. Louder shouts. Closer shots.

E. Z. jumped out of the loft and opened the barn door expecting to peer into darkness. Instead, he saw bright light. Large flames shot into the air. All the other farm buildings were on fire.

"Get down here as quick as you can!" E. Z. shouted to the others, and they followed him outside.

E. Z. barely could make out a rider heading from the direction of the fires carrying a torch in his hand. He turned to run back to the barn to rescue his map, hunting bag, and boots.

"No. Don't, E. Z.!" David begged.

"I can make it. You run to the woods and hide. Run to the woods!" E. Z. shouted at all the boys.

"I'm going with you," Isaiah said.

Jessie said, "We all are. We're a militia."

The boys followed E. Z. back into the barn and scrambled up the ladder to the loft. E. Z., Isaiah, and David put on their boots. The Sinking Creek boys wore no shoes in the summer.

E. Z. snatched the map and hunting bag. E. Z. took time to move the copy of the bandit's map to the bottom to hide it, and he put David's map on top above the bag of candy.

Nathaniel and Ezekiel went into action gathering up everything else. Then the boys jumped from the loft to a wagon loaded with hay below to make a quick escape. Except David. He began to climb down the ladder.

"Jump, David! I'll catch you," E. Z. yelled.

David jumped as E. Z. told him. David's weight knocked E. Z. to the ground, knocking the breath from E. Z.'s lungs. He gasped to force air into his chest. Isaiah helped E. Z. to his feet and pushed him toward the door.

When the boys ran out of the barn, they were relieved, to see U.S. soldiers standing outside. E. Z. first assumed that the soldiers had heard about the gang following them and had come to their rescue from Gordon's Ferry. The nearest soldier asked if everyone was out of the barn. E. Z. said "Yes, Sir."

That soldier waived his hand to motion two other soldiers forward. On signal, they threw their torches inside the barn. Fire trailed from the torches up the sides of the barn. The dry hay and wood exploded in flames. Fort Sinking Creek had fallen.

"What are you doing?" Jessie challenged the soldiers. A large man took him by the arm and pushed him aside.

The soldiers told the boys to go to their parents. The boys looked to the cabins where the parents were staying. Tall flames lapped from the doors and jumped from the roofs.

The soldiers assigned a young private to go with the boys to make certain they did not return to the barn. The private held his musket as if he would shoot the boys if they objected.

"Why are you burning our barn and houses?" Jessie asked again.

After Jessie refused to stay quiet, the soldier finally told him, "These farms are illegal. You built on Indian land."

"There are no Indian houses anywhere near here!" Jessie said.

"We don't want to do this. We are following orders," a young soldier said. Then, E. Z. recognized him as the sentinel they had seen at Gordon's Ferry. The soldiers were rangers from Gordon's Ferry as he had guessed.

When the boys saw their parents huddled together around a well, it was clear that they too had been turned out in the night. "Why did you wait for night?" E. Z. asked the soldier.

"We did not know whether you would try to shoot. It is safer to do this at night," the soldier said.

"Safer for who?" E. Z. protested.

The parents rushed beyond the soldiers to meet their sons to make certain that they were safe. Mr. Burton argued with one of the officers. "You have no right to do this without warning! You could have killed someone!"

The officer said, "We warned you."

"Nobody warned us!" Mr. Burton said.

"We told your agent several times. He assured us that he had warned you," the officer said.

"What agent?" Mr. Burton asked.

"Mr. Baron," the officer said as he rode away to check the fires.

"The Baron!" Mr. Burton said disgustedly.

"That is why he left in such a hurry before he showed us the land," Sarah said.

"Get in the wagon everybody!" Captain Stark shouted. Instead of panicking, the old soldier relied on his training. He had acted quickly to hitch the oxen to the wagon, put Major inside, and tied Esther to the back. "Let's get out of here before they try to burn the wagon too!" He looked with contempt at his fellow soldiers.

The boys took their place in the driver's seat with the captain. Captain Stark was not his usual jovial self. He told the boys to go back and sit in the wagon until they knew it was safe. E. Z. and David made their way back to their mother. Everyone looked confused or angry.

"Our beautiful farm," Sarah said. "It was too good to be true. We knew it was not ours. What was I thinking?"

"Can the other boys go with us? We'll make room," E. Z. asked.

"Their families may not be going to the same place. Some may go back East. They do not know where they will go. There has been no time to think about it," Sarah said.

Mr. Burton rode Esther. They still had Esther. At the first opportunity, they would plan to sell her for enough money to travel on to the Mississippi Territory and see what happened there.

The captain drove the wagon back toward The Devil's Backbone as fast as the oxen would take them. He seemed to ignore the rough ground that had made that leg of the trip physically painful. It only added to the emotional pain.

And as bad as everything seemed to be at that moment, the adventure was about to take a turn for the worse.

CHAPTER NINETEEN

Crossing the River

The glow of the fires from Sinking Creek gradually faded in the sky behind them as sunlight replaced it. No one in the wagon slept.

E. Z. wondered how his new friends were handling the events of the evening. E. Z. and his family had just arrived, but Sinking Creek had been his new friends' homes for over a year. His friends had invested their time and their work there.

"They knew they had no right to it" was what he was told. He could understand it. He had always been taught not to take someone else's property. What really bothered him was to see how disappointed his mother was and to lose his new friends. Only his mother understood how much trouble they faced.

As E. Z. stood in the wagon to get an idea of where they were, he thought he saw Jack riding his horse in the horizon behind them. That was one "friend" he would have preferred to leave behind on Sinking Creek. At least E. Z. could not see the bandit, or his ghost, following Jack.

Where would they go? E. Z. thought again of the wild-eyed boatmen's warning, "No one will ever hear from you again." They had been pulled back to The Devil's Backbone.

Supplies were low. The party was hungry and tired. The captain did not know where to find the next spring for water. Mr. Burton was unfamiliar with the area off the Natchez Trace.

Captain Stark stopped the wagon at a creek when he heard running water. The adults debated drinking creek water they knew was not safe to drink. No one really knew what was in it. But the children were becoming lifeless without water. They would have to take a chance. They skimmed off green scum with their hands and filled canteens.

"Careful not to scoop up things you can't identify," the captain said.

"If I had a bow, I could hunt," E. Z. said. "We could try catching a few fish."

"That's a good idea," the captain said. "Boys, take some hooks to the creek and see what you can find.

This stop was not the adventure of the past stops. It was a matter of survival. E. Z. quickly surveyed the creek but saw no fish. He spotted only a few minnows and crawfish. At least he did not see Jack either.

"Catch as many crawfish as you can," E. Z. told the boys. "We may have to eat them."

E. Z. waited for Isaiah to joke again about catching crawfish, but even Isaiah was in no joking mood. He knew they were in trouble.

The boys returned to the wagon with only a few fish and crawfish. Mr. Burton and Mr. Stewart had shot a few squirrels. E. Z. and Isaiah built a small campfire. The mothers did the best they could. They made a soup to make the meat go further. They had no choice but to use the creek water. At least the smell was savory.

Hannah picked at her soup. Mary encouraged her, "Don't think about it. Just eat it. You need something in your stomach."

Captain Stark attempted to cheer the party. "Many times, we had little food in the war. It was tough, but we survived. We will survive this time too. You'll see. Not long from now, we will all look back and understand how things were never as bleak as they seem now."

The travelers sat around the fire from force of habit, but no one was in a mood to talk. There was a sense that they were drifting like the boat on the Cumberland River. "[T]his boat's a'takin you," E. Z. could hear the boatman say in his mind.

The next morning everyone awoke feeling sick. Mr. Burton said that he had been up most of the night. David also had gotten up sick in the night.

The women were surprised to find a small bag of flour by the campfire. "Where did that come from?" Sarah asked.

Sarah looked around for any clue, but no one could imagine how it suddenly had appeared. She opened the bag and smelled it. The flour was fresh. She accepted it and began making biscuits. The creek water was all she had.

Everyone tried to eat some of the biscuits. A few found they could not eat anything. "Just a little," Mary prodded Hannah.

"According to the map, the Natchez Trace should not be far ahead. Then, we will reach the Tennessee River. Colbert's Ferry is there. Chief Colbert has a whole settlement on the other side of the river. We should be able to find what we need there," Mr. Burton said.

"How will we pay for anything?" Sarah asked.

"Esther. We will sell Esther," he said. The horse looked at him when she heard her name.

Captain Stark said before he thought, "In the war, we ate horses when we had nothing else. Sometimes you have to make sacrifices for the good of the whole."

Mary scolded him. "Papa. The children."

He looked at Hannah's worried face and added, "But this horse is far more valuable doing her work."

As the party finally reached the Natchez Trace and traveled on down the road, the rocking and swaying of the wagon only made everyone feel worse. One by one, they asked Captain Stark to stop so that they could get off and throw up. One person's groans were reflected by another's. None of them was well enough to cheer the others.

The boys begged to ride up front again, and their mothers finally agreed. Major seemed to be the only one who felt well. He was recovering, and he could not understand why everyone else was not as energetic as they had been.

"How about another candy distribution to the troops?" the captain said, trying to take the children's minds off their condition. No one was interested.

The person who had left the bag of flour was still a mystery. That discussion would have to wait. Everyone was too queasy to discuss food.

David's head dropped and he nearly passed out. E. Z. took hold of David's shirt to keep him steady on the wagon seat. He decided that it was safer for David to ride in the wagon, where his mother could watch him. Sarah said that she would make him talk every few miles to make sure that he was still alert.

Near dark, the wagon gradually began to descend the ridge hill. A loud roaring sound greeted the party. This time, the sound was from water instead of fire. They had made it to the Tennessee River.

The blast of noise came from the lower shoals or shallows where the water roared as it passed through the rocks jutting out of the bed of the river. In summer, the water was low enough that a brave man could walk across the slick rocks. The foolish took a chance of losing balance and being dashed against rocks downstream.

Lights from Colbert's inn were in view across the river. It was one of several buildings that appeared to be part of the small town that Mr. Burton had described. E. Z. could see silhouettes of people walking between them. If the party could only get across the river, they should be safe and find food and shelter.

The party agreed on a plan to wait for Colbert's ferry boat to come to take them across the water. As the post rider Donley had warned them, if they arrived late in the day, they would have to camp overnight on the north bank and wait for Colbert to bring the ferry boat the next day. Mr. Burton tried shouting for Colbert's servants across the river, but his voice was drowned out by the sound of the water.

"We'll have to make camp here tonight," he said.

"What about the bandits they told us about? Won't they know we are here?" E. Z. asked.

"We cannot swim across. We will have to wait until the ferry boat crosses to pick us up," Mr. Burton said.

No one felt up to searching for wood to build a fire. Maybe the darkness would help them avoid drawing attention to the campsite. A few other campfires could be seen along the north riverbank, but there was no way of knowing who was camped by them.

"David!" Sarah shouted. "David!"

"What's wrong?" Mr. Burton asked.

"He is not answering me! His eyes look strange!" she said.

Mr. Burton climbed up into the wagon and lifted David off. Sarah made a pallet for him. Mr. Stewart brought some straw to put underneath him. Sarah told E. Z. to go down to the river and fetch some water to boil. David seemed to have fever.

E. Z. dashed toward the river. He tried yelling again to get the attention of anyone across the water. No one could hear him.

He looked for any way across, even counting the rocks jutting out of the water to see how many it would take to cross on foot. If he had to, he would try.

E. Z.'s shouting did draw the attention of men at one of the tents on the north riverbank a few hundred yards from where Captain Stark was setting camp. The men came out of the tent and looked at the party that they had not noticed.

E. Z. ran back to the temporary camp with the bucket of water. He saw Sarah rubbing David's head and begging him to talk to her. She dampened a piece of cloth in the bucket and placed it on David's head.

Captain Stark examined him. "I think he just has not had enough good water. He will be fine." Turning to E. Z. and Isaiah, he said, "Boys, I know it is dark, but run back up the hill and see if you can find a spring up there to get some fresh water to drink. Take a bucket. Watch for snakes."

E. Z. and Isaiah found their way in the light of a half-moon to the top of the hill. There was a spring as the captain had suggested. As they walked back toward camp, E. Z. saw men rounding up their horses near one of the campfires.

Other men ran out of their tents and started to gather. They began looking toward the party's camp. Those men must have been the bandits who preyed on travelers at the river. Or they could have been the bandits who had followed the party from Nashville, waiting for their last chance. E. Z. saw three men wearing white linen clothes. He also thought one man was wearing a patch over his eye. That man was talking with a man with long, stringy hair.

The boys ran back to camp and told the adults. Mr. Burton walked to where he could see the horses and count them. He said that it appeared that the men were saddling their horses, preparing to ride. They had only a few minutes to escape.

"Where can we go? If we turn back up the road, they will catch us," Captain Stark said.

"The river is our only escape. We have to try to cross the river," Mr. Burton said.

"We can't move David. He is too ill," Sarah said.

Mr. Burton put both hands on Sarah's arms, "David cannot stay here. I will carry him. Ezekiel, you help your mother."

"We can't leave!" Mary objected frantically. She looked at Mr. Stewart and her voice was not soft this time. "John, you tell them we can't leave." No one seemed to know what she was talking about, but E. Z. noticed that she was looking at her father. The captain was too old to cross the river by walking on the rocks. "We can't leave!" she cried as she lowered her head into her hands.

Captain Stark realized her objections. "No. You have to go. I will stay here. Somebody must guard the wagon. Hand me my gun and powder."

"No!" Mary continued. "John, you tell them there is safety in numbers. We can't leave Papa."

Mr. Stewart took Mary's hand and patted it. "We have to think about Hannah and Isaiah. They cannot stay. They will need parents, and we cannot stay."

"This is all your fault," Mary said as she pushed Mr. Stewart's hand aside and began to gather a few belongings in a sack to take with them.

Mr. Stewart put his hand over the sack. "Mary, we won't be able to take anything with us across the river."

"Hurry! There is no time!" Mr. Burton said, grunting as he picked up David and placed him over his shoulder. "Captain Stark...." He stopped when he could think of nothing to say to the old soldier they were abandoning to a likely death.

Captain Stark pushed them forward. "Go! Go while you have time! When you reach the other side, send the ferry boat back for me. I'll hold them off until then."

Mary, Isaiah, and Hannah rushed up to hug the captain, and then turned to make their way in the darkness down toward the river. Isaiah and E. Z. looked back to see the captain standing at attention near the wagon like the good soldier he was.

Major followed the party to the river. E. Z. stooped down and patted the dog on the head. "You can't go with us, boy. You won't make it across the river. It's too wide. Go back and help the captain." E. Z. pointed to the captain.

Rejected, Major lowered his head and walked back slowly. The dog turned his head every few steps to see if E. Z. had changed his mind.

"Do you want me to carry David across the river?" E. Z. asked Mr. Burton.

"I have him. You hold on to your mother!" Mr. Burton said.

Captain Stark began to play his fiddle to draw attention away from the party crossing the river. He shouted using different voices to make it appear that there still were several people in camp. He clapped his hands to shoo Esther away from the camp to create another diversion. Major did his part by barking and growling.

"Pull off your boots! The rocks will be slick," Mr. Burton said.

E. Z. quickly looked inside the hunting bag he had snatched as they ran from camp. It also contained the last money Sarah had left. There was not much. The Spanish coin from Gordon's Ferry was probably worth more. Then there were the maps and candy. E. Z. hung the bag around his neck. "Here, take this. You'll need it," he heard the voice of the wild-eyed boatman in his mind.

E. Z. stepped down into the water, balanced himself out on the first rock, and held his hand for his mother. The swift water roared around them. The water looked dark and bottomless. "No one will ever hear from you again" the voice in his head kept repeating.

Mr. Stewart was doing the same for his family. They slowly balanced themselves on the closest rocks.

Mr. Burton had a tougher time carrying David. He did not have a counterweight to keep his balance. Mr. Burton stopped to study the rocks, unsure how to move forward.

E. Z. kept a watch on his brother. He saw Mr. Burton's challenge in keeping his balance. E. Z. also noticed that several of the rocks were too far apart to walk across above the surface. They had not been able to see the spaces between the rocks from the riverbank. The water was too swift to walk between them. Besides, in the dark, they had no way to know how deep the river was to get their footing if they slipped.

"We have to go back!" E. Z. said to Mr. Burton, drowned out by the roar of the water. Then louder, motioning with his hands. "Go back!"

Mr. Burton had no choice. E. Z. was already leading his mother back to shore. The Stewart family saw them returning to shore and followed them back.

As the party reached the riverbank, they discovered that it had been easier to go down into the river than to climb out of it. The steep bank was muddy and slick. It took E. Z. several tries to climb up. Then, E. Z. extended his hand to help the others. He had to climb halfway down and dig his feet into the mud to get a footing to help Mr. Burton lift David.

"What do we do now?" Mr. Stewart shouted. He glanced back to see that men from the other campsites were riding horses in their direction. The men did not appear to be rushing to rescue the travelers.

E. Z. pointed to a post on the riverbank. "I spotted the chains for the ferry up there. We can hold on to them and walk or swim across."

"Isaiah and Hannah can't swim," Mr. Stewart said.

"I can now, Pa," Isaiah said. "E. Z. taught me."

"I don't know if we are strong enough, but hold on to Hannah and we'll try," Mary said.

E. Z. led the party to the north crossing point for the ferry and showed them the chains. He gripped Sarah's hand with one of his hands and placed his other on the chain. They slowly walked from shore.

On the third step, E. Z. discovered that the riverbed was too deep, and he went underwater. He remembered the boatman's stories of arms pulling boys down to drown them, and he kicked his feet in case. Even with the sudden surprise of water filling his ears, E. Z. held fast to the chain and his mother. He shouted to the party that they would have to hold tight to the chain.

Mr. Burton was next. David was a heavy weight, but Mr. Burton was strong. Still, it took nearly all his strength to keep David's head above the water.

Mr. Stewart followed. He told Hannah to place her arms around his head and not let go. Isaiah held on to his mother.

The river was nearly a mile wide, even in summer. The swift river current made the progression across the river even slower. Much of the party's energy was spent holding onto the chain and fighting the rushing water to keep from being swept away. Everyone began to lose their strength before reaching the midway point.

Sarah panted as she had on the hill near Bentontown. "I don't think I can hold on… E. Z., let me go… You will get across faster …without me."

She had never called him "E. Z." It was clear that she had little energy left to talk.

"No, Ma. I'm not letting go!" E. Z. shouted.

"Hold on, Sarah!" Mr. Burton shouted for encouragement.

"Let us just…stop… here a moment… I will see if I can… catch my breath," she gasped.

One of the men on horseback fired a shot that hit the water near Mr. Burton.

"We need to move faster," Mr. Burton said.

E. Z. spotted a tall figure moving on the Colbert's south shore of the river. When the figure heard the shot and saw what was happening, he turned and began motioning toward the buildings.

Within seconds, several other men ran out of the buildings toward the ferry boat anchored by the chains. The men brought out long poles like those the boatmen had used on the Cumberland and began pushing the boat.

The men on horseback saw the ferry boat coming across the river, and they stopped.

"Look, Ma! They're coming! The boat's coming! Don't let go!" E. Z. shouted.

Sarah had greater trouble breathing. The current was too much for her. Her face was turning gray in the pale moonlight, and her hand began to lose its grip with E. Z.'s.

"The boat...is moving...so slow," Sarah wheezed. "It will not get here...in time."

"It will. Just hang on! Do you feel a rock you can put your feet on?" E. Z. shouted.

"No.... just water," she responded weakly.

E. Z. began to move his legs to see if he could position them on a rock. "Here! Here is one! Try moving over a little toward me."

Sarah began to pull away. E. Z. found a reserve of strength to pull her closer.

Mr. Burton struggled with David. Mr. Burton, too, was becoming weak and his arms began shaking. A couple times, David's head went underwater. E. Z. searched with his legs for another rock for Mr. Burton to stand on.

"Here! There's a rock over here!" E. Z. shouted. Mr. Burton moved slowly toward the rock.

The Stewarts had also come to a complete stop. Isaiah held on to his mother. Hannah was scared and crying.

As the ferry boat approached, three black boatmen rushed over to the side to help the party aboard. E. Z. tried to lift himself onto the boat and pull his mother up, but his tired muscles failed him. He lost the grip of his mother's hand.

Sarah was swept up in the current that propelled her backwards toward a rock jutting out of the river. E. Z. swam back to catch her, but he was too slow. Sarah struck the rock hard.

E. Z. swam faster and reached his mother just in time to take hold of her arm to keep her from being lost forever downstream.

The boatmen held out a pole. E. Z. latched onto it and pulled his way back to the boat, holding Sarah's head just above the water. E. Z. found a new source of strength in the fear that he would lose her. The muscled boatmen had no trouble pulling the thin woman up on the boat and laying her gently on the floor.

Two of the boatmen ran to the side to help pull David out of the water. When Mr. Burton saw that David was onboard the platform, he relaxed and almost lost his grip. E. Z. swam over to staunch Mr. Burton's shoulder to keep him from being swept backward into the rush like his mother.

The boatmen then began to pull the rest of the party aboard the ferry boat. Mr. Stewart insisted that Hannah be the first of their family to board. She refused to let go of him. Her arms were locked so firmly around his head that they had to pry them apart.

When the travelers were laid on the floor of the ferry boat, their bodies went limp from exhaustion. The boatmen shouted above the roar to encourage each other quickly to pull in the rest.

E. Z. was the last to be pulled aboard. He lay on his back and stared up at the stars in the clear night sky. They seemed so fixed, so peaceful in contrast to the panic that had been going on around him.

E. Z. turned his head to see his mother. Her eyes were nearly closed, and she was taking heavy breaths. From the part of Sarah's eyes that were visible, she seemed to be staring at E. Z. from as far away as those peaceful stars in the sky.

"We made it, Ma. David's here, too."

When Sarah heard E. Z.'s distant voice that her sons were safe, her eyes shut completely.

E. Z. allowed his eyes to close for a moment and saw himself floating peacefully on the boat on the Cumberland in the sunshine. "Never hear from…Never" the wild boatman's voice repeated, then interrupted, "HERE?"

E. Z. opened his eyes. "What?"

It was the ferry boatman. "EVERYBODY HERE?"

E. Z. tried to sit up but could manage only to raise his chest by leaning on his elbow. He looked around and saw everyone. Totally exhausted and wet. They were all there. "All here," he said.

Above the roar, gunfire rang from the north bank. Captain Stark! The captain and Major were not there safe aboard the boat. E. Z. started to ask one of the ferrymen to return for them, but then, he lost consciousness.

CHAPTER TWENTY

Transition to a New World

When E. Z. opened his eyes again, he was inside a room. A lamp was flickering its light on the ceiling. Someone had put him to bed. David was beside him.

The tall figure he had seen on shore was standing at his bedside examining the bead bracelet on his wrist. The man turned and left the room. E. Z. noticed that the man had long, straight, black hair that hung down below his shoulders.

A few minutes later, Samuel, one of the Chickasaw boys he had seen at McLish's, came into the room. The boy smiled, "E. Z. Friend. Brother." E. Z. thought he was dreaming again and that he was back at McLish's.

"Samuel?....What are you doing here? …. Where am I?" E. Z. asked.

"Colbert's house. You cross the water." Samuel said.

E. Z. remembered everything now. He sat up and looked at David. David's eyes were closed. E. Z. jostled David's shoulder with his hand. David barely opened his eyes. In a groggy, hoarse voice, David said, "What are you looking at? Go back to sleep."

"David!" E. Z. shouted and reached down to hug his brother.

"Get off. I'm too tired to wrestle," David said as he pushed him away.

Then E. Z. thought of his mother. He climbed out of bed and started to put on his wet clothes. Samuel showed him Chickasaw leggings and a dry calico shirt that had been laid out for him. He put them on instead.

Samuel laughed. "You look Chikasha now. Like true warrior."

"Why are we sleeping inside?" E. Z. asked.

"Others sleep on porches till you better." Samuel said.

When the travelers were brought in, they were all too weak to defend themselves from any critters or bandits that came up in the night. Inside was safer even if it was warm. Colbert's house had glass windows, a luxury in The Wilderness, that could be opened to let in a river breeze.

E. Z. walked barefooted out to the porch, which was lit with lanterns on tables. Mr. Burton was there, sitting in a cane-bottom chair next to a closed door. He appeared to be deep in thought.

Mr. Stewart came out of another room. He said that Mary and his children were resting. Mr. Stewart asked about Sarah. Mr. Burton only shook his head.

"Where's Ma?" E. Z. blurted out in fear.

Mr. Burton lifted his head and turned to E. Z. Mr. Burton's normally confident face looked pained and sad. He did not speak. He nodded to the shut door to the side of him.

E. Z. braced himself and opened the door. A dim lamp lit the room. Sarah was lying on a bed with her eyes closed. She was no longer breathing heavily like she was the last time E. Z. had seen her on the boat.

A small Chickasaw woman came up behind E. Z. and with a small push moved him to the side as she entered the room. The woman, who appeared to be more than a hundred years old, placed her wrinkled hand on Sarah's forehead. The woman then took a pot she carried and poured a hot liquid into a cup. A strong odor from the liquid filled the room. The woman picked up a feather, dipped it in the cup, and cooled the liquid by blowing on it. The woman said something E. Z. did not understand as she placed a little of the liquid on Sarah's lips.

The old woman stayed at Sarah's side. She appeared to be working with something, but her back was turned to E. Z.

"You cannot see." Samuel said just behind E. Z. He had followed him. "Only medicine people can know." Samuel stepped in front of E. Z. to guide him out and shut the door.

"How is David?" Mr. Burton asked.

"He's awake. Thank you for saving him. He would have been too heavy for me," E. Z. said.

Mr. Burton acknowledged E. Z.'s thanks with a small nod. "One of the women brought some hominy soup. It is over there on the table. Do not take too much. You have not had much to eat in a couple days, and if you eat too much at one time, it will make you sick." It is what E. Z.'s mother would have told him.

E. Z. poured some soup into a bowl and took it to the side of the porch to eat where there was a breeze and where he could think. He wondered what would happen if Sarah died. They would be alone.

He had seen orphaned children back home who were forced to become indentured servants or apprentices to survive. Orphans had to work for strangers for years as they learned a trade and earned their keep. But then, he and David would have to get back home first. No, they had no home now.

Colbert's Inn was perched on a hill overlooking the Tennessee River. As E. Z. sat on the porch eating the soup, he could look across the river to the north bank and see that campfires were still burning. Captain Stark, Major, Esther, nor the wagon was anywhere in sight. Hearing the rushing water reminded E. Z. how close they all had come to being lost.

Samuel had been standing back, uncertain what to say. He walked over and sat beside E. Z.

"You better?" Samuel asked.

"This food helps. It's good. I'm just very tired. If Ma recovers, we'll all be fine, but I'm not sure where we'll go," E. Z. said.

"Maybe you stay here," Samuel suggested.

"We may have to stay awhile and work off our bill. We have lost almost all our money. Not that we had much, but we could take care of ourselves. Now....," E. Z. hesitated. A boy normally did not have to worry about those things, but without his mother, it would be E. Z.'s responsibility. He had determined at McLish's that it was time he began thinking like a man.

"They take care of you here. No charge," Samuel said.

"No charge?"

"You friend, brother. Colbert not charge people with no money. You ask him," Samuel said.

"Ma will not accept charity. She will insist that we work for what we get," E. Z. said.

"People come here sick, no money. No charge," Samuel said. "You have much money—big charge." Samuel laughed.

"No, I can work. I will feel up to doing some chores tomorrow. It may take a few days before I can work hard. David will work, too.... Please... just tell your people to take care of our Ma ... and....don't...let her............. die."

E. Z. lowered and turned his head to hide his tears. He was mad at himself for crying. But he was exhausted, and he could not imagine life without his mother or trying to survive on his own. Especially in The Wilderness.

There was David to think of, too. He would raise his brother until he was old enough to survive on his own.

A million thoughts ran through E. Z.'s mind as he tried to make sense of everything that had happened. He had forgotten that his mother was not awake to see after David. He rose to pour a bowl of soup to take his brother and then turned to return to their room.

"Tomorrow?" he asked Samuel.

Samuel smiled at the prospect of a new day and time to spend with his new friend. "*Ona*. Tomorrow."

CHAPTER TWENTY-ONE

Tomorrow

The next morning, the sun shone through the window and lit up the hunting bag. It was the first thing E. Z. saw as he opened his eyes. The map!

E. Z. sprang out of bed thinking that someone had probably already searched through the hunting bag. He was surprised to see the map folded up in the bottom. David's map of the Cumberland River that E. Z. had placed on top was missing.

"Is it there?" David asked, as he raised up.

"Yes," E. Z. said. But river water had soaked through the candy bag. Wet candy had leaked through the bag and stuck to the map, making it all appear to be candy. The wet candy had saved the map by hiding it. E. Z. pried the candy off the map. As E. Z. held the candy in his hand, he thought of Captain Stark.

The candy was part of the life and the good times of the world he had left behind when he crossed the river. Now, the candy was worthless.

Still, E. Z. had the map. It was damp. But as he opened it, he could see that it was only slightly smudged.

They had lost everything of any value, but each other and the map. E. Z. did not even have boots to put it in now. Maybe the Indians would show him how to sew some moccasins.

E. Z. saw a small crack between the logs in the corner of the room. He folded the map twice and stuffed it inside.

After dressing quickly in his new Chickasaw clothes, E. Z. left David and stepped out to see his mother. Mr. Burton was still seated in the same chair. But now it leaned back against the wall on two legs so that he was reclining. His head was low, and his hat was pulled down over his eyes to keep out the sunlight. He was asleep.

E. Z. studied the man who had risked his life to save his brother. If E. Z. could learn to trust Mr. Burton, he would have hundreds of questions for him.

"Is he your daddy?" asked an enslaved woman putting out a breakfast spread.

"No, Ma'am. Why?" E. Z. asked.

"The only time that man left that chair was to look in on you two. About every hour. I thought he was your daddy," she said. "I will take the young one some dry clothes. We have yours dryin' in the sun."

"Thank you." Motioning to the door of his mother's room, E. Z. asked, "May I go in?"

"Yes. But don't you stay long. Then come out and get some breakfast, child," the woman said kindly.

E. Z. opened the door to his mother's room. The medicine woman was still there keeping watch over Sarah. The old woman briefly looked up to stare at E. Z., then lowered her head without speaking.

E. Z. put his hand on his mother's arm. Sarah opened her eyes and barely above a whisper said, "Ezekiel. You are safe. David?"

"Yes, Ma'am. He's safe too. He's fine."

Sarah attempted to squeeze E. Z.'s hand. Then she added, "Mr. Burton?"

"He's outside. He's asleep. The Stewarts are fine too," he said quietly, remembering Captain Stark, but not mentioning him. Sarah smiled and closed her eyes.

The medicine woman looked up again and gave E. Z. a glance that told him to leave.

When E. Z. walked outside, he saw that the Stewart family had just sat down to breakfast. Mary and Hanna were quietly sobbing. Mr. Stewart had talked to some men at the ferry about sending out a party to search for Captain Stark as soon as they arrived at the north bank.

As Isaiah and Hannah asked about David, he walked outside wearing his own Chickasaw clothing. The shirt was too small. The bottom of the shirt did not cover his navel.

Hannah stopped crying and laughed when she saw him. She was better, too.

Sitting around familiar aromas of breakfast in the sun, for the moment, restored a feeling of something that had not changed. The boys even tried telling a few jokes. Not that they felt like humor; they needed something to be normal until they figured everything else out. It would be a long time before the adults were ready for jokes.

Samuel came outside to where the group was eating. He pulled E. Z. aside. "I tell them you work. You like horses?"

"We do," all the other boys said almost at the same time.

Samuel said, "This way. I show you."

E. Z., David, and Isaiah followed Samuel away from the river. It was the first time E. Z. had noticed his surroundings at Colbert's. Wild peacocks ran around the yard, clacking and spreading their shimmering wings.

Behind the house there was a cabin village. Herds of cattle grazed in some fields. Other fields were covered with cotton plants. Boats traveling the river docked at the ferry below and unloaded goods into large storehouses.

E. Z. had thought McLish's Inn was large. No place he had seen compared to this. The buildings looked like the settlements in Tennessee. The main difference was that most of the people at Colbert's were either Chickasaws, their slaves, travelers or boatmen who stayed there.

As the boys walked around a small hill, E. Z. spotted another pasture. Wild horses grazed there. There were Appaloosas, of course, but also mustangs. Young colts bolted through the fields even though nothing was chasing them. It was a beautiful sight.

For the moment, the excitement of watching the horses took the boys' attention away from their troubles.

Young Chickasaw men ran into the pasture, jumped on the backs of the running horses, and began riding them. E. Z. noticed how the men used their legs to turn the horses rather than using bridles as white men did.

"How do they do that?" David asked in amazement. The Indian riders had somehow learned how to ride in sync with the horses as if they were one.

Samuel said, "It is their work. They ride horses."

"That's all they do?" E. Z. asked.

"They ride in war, too," Samuel said.

"Don't they work in the fields?" Isaiah asked.

"Them men? No!" Samuel laughed. "That is work for women here."

Isaiah asked, "Remember how those soldiers at Gordon's Ferry spent their time mending uniforms and fixing up buildings?"

"That's all they did until they set our fort on fire," David said.

Isaiah joked, "I am officially resigning my commission as a soldier. I have decided that I would rather be a Chickasaw warrior."

E. Z. nodded in agreement as he turned in a complete circle trying to take it all in. "Colbert must be the richest man in the whole world!"

Could Colbert's be where the map led? E. Z. could not imagine more treasure in one place.

Maybe the old boatman had been correct. Maybe no one would ever hear from E. Z. again. The Indian nation looked so promising that he might never want to leave.

Follow E. Z.'s next chapter in the *Fighting The Devil's Backbone* series and other work by Tony L. Turnbow at tonyturnbow.com

AUTHOR'S NOTE

A s a young boy, I was fascinated by stories my great aunts and uncles told of the world that their great-grandparents experienced. That world was Tennessee and the Natchez Trace in the early 1800's. My older family members' and their neighbors' customs had changed little from the time their ancestors settled in Tennessee. I not only heard about that distant world—I experienced some of it through their culture.

Older family members told me about ancestors who fought under General George Washington in the American Revolution. Then too, there were ancestors who were parents of the notorious John Murrell, one of the bandits on the Natchez Trace. "We don't talk about *him*," is all my great-aunt would tell curious outsiders. In private, though, she delighted in relating how just the mention of the family connection to "Murrell" scared off marauders during the Civil War.

In the days before radio, television, and the internet, families entertained each other by telling stories. Adults also entertained themselves by scaring children with tall tales of ghosts, witches, supernatural creatures, and Indian warriors. Over time, those stories became intertwined with true accounts, as if both actually occurred.

When I was old enough to research more about the Natchez Trace, I discovered equally fascinating stories of other people who may have passed by my family's farm on the old Natchez Trace Indian trail. I am incorporating a few of those stories into this series through the lives of the fictional characters.

I also had the opportunity to meet descendants of Southeastern American Indian leaders. (I use the term "Indian" rather than "Native American," because that is the preference of the Indian friends I have made.) They taught me about the different perspectives of their cultures, and I learned how much the Indians and settlers learned from each other. The history of the Natchez Trace makes no sense unless there is an understanding of the Indian history and perspective.

History is not boring, and certainly it is not irrelevant to our lives. Ultimately, history is the story of people and their hopes, their fears, and their struggles. There is much we can learn from the people who lived in earlier times. How they faced challenges like ours and whether they succeeded or failed in their attempts is worth the time to study. History helps us understand the present.

When I completed my first book, the non-fiction *Hardened to Hickory: The Missing Chapter in Andrew Jackson's Life*, a good friend suggested that I write a fictional series to share the history I have learned with young readers. Not just names and dates, but the good stuff—the stories of people. My hope is that this story drawn from snippets of history I learned about the Natchez Trace will encourage readers to explore the history of the places all around us. And, that the exploration of history will provide the reader an understanding of the present.

ABOUT THE AUTHOR

Tony L. Turnbow is the author of the non-fiction *Hardened to Hickory: The Missing Chapter in Andrew Jackson's Life*. He has studied the history of the Old Natchez Trace for more than 30 years.

He practices law in Franklin, Tennessee. With a Bachelor of Arts and a concentration in southern U.S. history from Vanderbilt University and a Juris Doctorate from the University of Tennessee College of Law, he has continued to use his training to explore unpublished primary sources about the Natchez Trace. He authored "The Natchez Trace in the War of 1812" in *The Journal of Mississippi History*, and he has published articles in the *Tennessee Historical Quarterly* and the Lewis and Clark Trail Heritage Foundation journal "We Proceeded On." He also wrote a full-length play "Inquest on the Natchez Trace" about the mysterious death of explorer Meriwether Lewis.

Mr. Turnbow represented the Natchez Trace Parkway Association on the Tennessee War of 1812 Bicentennial Commission, and he was the recipient of the Tennessee Society U.S. Daughters of 1812 "Spirit of 1812" award. He enjoys telling the stories of the old Natchez Trace.